Throwback
THE CHAOS LOOP

Peter Lerangis

Throwback

THE CHAOS LOOP

HARPER
An Imprint of HarperCollins Publishers

To the memory of Kurt Messerschmidt,
whose story of bravery, sacrifice, and grit in escaping
the Nazis is a great inspiration to me.
—P.L.

1

Corey Fletcher was two hours early, but about three minutes late.

Well, later than he wanted to be, anyway. He was still getting the hang of time-hopping.

As he rounded the corner toward the 96th Street station, he scooted around his neighbor, Walter Preston. Walter's black Lab, Bailey, wagged his tail at the sight of Corey, but Corey was in too much of a hurry to say hello. Sprinting down the subway stairs, he could hear the rumble of the uptown train approaching. The station clock said 4:17. In one minute the train would be in the station, and the doors would open. At that moment, his sister, Zenobia, would be attacked.

He knew all this, because it had already happened.

She had come home crying. Corey had felt so angry and frustrated that he hadn't been with her.

That's why he had traveled to the *before*. Before the incident happened. Before his sister was hurt. Because he was going to change things. He was going to thwart that attack.

His watch beeped 6:17, but he ignored that. Messing with time could make your head spin. He'd aimed to get here just a few minutes earlier, with enough time to think of a plan. But he was late. It hadn't worked exactly the way he wanted. It hardly ever did.

He'd just have to wing it now.

"An uptown train is entering the station . . ." came a recorded voice from below. "Please stand clear of the platform edge. . . ."

He raced for the turnstile, nearly knocking over a girl with blue hair as she fumbled in her pocket for a MetroCard. Shouting a hurried apology, he plowed past her. Even though he'd grown five inches that year and had trouble with coordination, he flew down the steps three at a time.

The train shoved air through the tunnel as it entered the station. It created a warm breeze that smelled of dust and stale pee. Corey cast a quick glance left and right. The platform was nearly empty, so he crouched as close to the edge as he could. He could predict the exact spot where Zenobia would exit. She always did the same thing, every single trip. She sat near the door closest to the turnstiles, so she could be the first person out of the train and up the stairs. She was so competitive.

Corey covered his ears against the shriek of the brakes. Several cars slid past him as the train slowed to a stop. Through the window he could see Zenobia in the train, sitting on an orange seat, tapping on her phone. He could see her mop of dark brown hair, even thicker than his own. The fluorescent subway lights made her glasses glint. She hated wearing those glasses.

Most people would be texting or posting, but not Zenobia. Even though she was still in high school, she was writing her memoir, which she was convinced would make her rich and famous. And she wasn't watching anything around her. Or anyone. Her back-pack was resting beside her on the seat, her right arm hooked through one of the straps.

She definitely did not see the guy sitting at the other end of the bench, wearing the black ski mask.

"This stop is . . . Ninety-Sixth Street . . ." chimed a voice from inside the car.

The train clunked to a halt and the door noisily

3

slid open. The black-mask guy pulled out a knife. In a quick move like a dancer, he spun toward Zenobia and sliced through the backpack strap that was hooked to her arm.

As he pulled the pack away, she let out a piercing shriek. Her phone clattered to the floor. The attacker scooped it up as he ran toward the door.

"Give it back, you creep!" Zenobia screamed, although honestly, she used a stronger word than *creep*. She lunged for him, managing to grab the back of the guy's jacket. It was enough to keep him inside the train car, but his momentum pulled her onto the floor behind him.

Now. Don't think!

Trying to be a hero was crazy, and Corey knew it. The guy had a weapon. Also, Corey had never played football, never taken a martial arts class, and hadn't the faintest idea how to attack someone.

As the man shook off Zenobia and ran for the door, Corey did the first thing that came to mind.

He ducked.

The attacker didn't expect a body just outside the door. His midsection caught Corey in the shoulders. Both of them tumbled to the ground in the doorway. Corey tried to push the guy away, but the doors slid shut on either side. They lurched open and closed, again and again, banging against their bodies with an insistent thump-thump-thump.

"Let the doors go!" a voice barked over the loudspeaker.

With a grunt, the attacker pushed Corey away and sprang to his feet.

But Zenobia jumped at him, grabbing for her pack. "Give that back!" she shouted.

Off-balance, the man stumbled back into the car. The pack slipped off his shoulders and out of Zenobia's hands, landing on the floor. Corey scooped it up and stood in the doorway, making sure it stayed open. "Hurry!" he shouted to his sister.

As Zenobia slipped past him, Corey spotted the blue-haired girl. She had entered the car through another door and was standing a few feet away, aiming her phone at the scene. But at the moment, her face was turning ashen with fright.

The attacker was lurching toward Corey with the knife.

No time to think. Corey lashed out with a kick. His heel caught the guy square in the knee, causing the man's head to jerk back and hit a metal pole. He slumped slowly downward again, moaning.

"Whoa," said the blue-haired girl.

"Did *you* do that?" Zenobia said.

"Let go of the doors!" came the conductor's voice as the door banged against Corey again.

He backed out of the car and onto the platform. Through the open doors, he caught a glimpse of the blue-haired girl, phone to her side, staring downward with her mouth hanging open.

"Next stop, One Hundred and Third . . ." came an announcement.

On the train floor, their attacker was groaning for help. "Knife . . ." he called out, reaching toward the blue-haired girl. "Fell . . . on knife . . ."

As the doors slid slowly shut, Corey could see a trickle of dark liquid oozing out from underneath his body.

2

"I still don't understand why you left me, Corey," Zenobia said.

Corey stared at the TV. The den was crowded. Watching the 7:00 local news after dinner was a family tradition. Corey's dad's parents, aka Papou and Yiayia, sat in matching leather reclining chairs. They lived in the same brownstone. His other grandmother, on his mom's side, was in a wheelchair, visiting from the elder-care facility on West End Avenue. Mutti didn't speak much anymore, and sometimes she didn't know where she was. She moaned and cried a lot, but right now her eyes were glued to the TV screen.

What happened in the subway had caught the attention of the press. When the reporters had gotten there, the train had still been in the station. A crowd of passengers had gathered around the blue-haired girl and the attacker. By that time Zenobia was gone.

Corey had left before her, slipping away when she wasn't looking to get back to the present. "I left because I heard a siren," Corey said. It was a lie, and not a very good one. "Like I told you. I followed them down Ninety-Fifth Street. Sorry."

"You couldn't have just called nine-one-one?" Zenobia asked.

"*Paithi mou,* Corey was trying to help," Papou said.

"I know, I know." Zenobia took Corey's hand and kissed him on the cheek. Normally that kind of behavior would have sent Corey away screaming, but he felt numb. It was one thing to save Zenobia. It was a whole other thing to cause a man to fall on a knife, even a bad guy. Corey hoped he hadn't died. There was nothing about the incident on his news app.

Corey's phone dinged and he quickly glanced at a text notification.

Leila Sharp

can u meet me RIGHT NOW in the park?
u test me for my AP German vocab quiz
tmw & ill treat u to mila café

He texted back a quick no. Leila was his best friend. She was also the only thirteen-year-old he knew who was taking AP German. But that was because her dad and mom were descended from Germans and her family spoke the language while she was growing up. Anyway, she would have to wait. Everything would have to wait until he figured this out.

His mind raced. There were options if the guy *had* died. Corey could do the whole thing again. He could go back even earlier in time and get it right. He could get the police involved in advance. If they were set up for action, waiting at the station, then the masked guy would have to give himself up. The fight wouldn't happen.

That was the advantage of being a Throwback. You had the power to redo anything. Infinitely. All Corey would need was a chance to get away.

"Mama, is that you?" whispered Mutti, as an urgent-looking woman with beautiful hair appeared on the screen.

"No, Mutti," Corey's mom said, taking her hand. "It's only a newscaster."

"This is Carla Hasty with breaking news," the TV woman said. "This afternoon, a potential thief on the C train received a shock, thanks to a young hero named Trilby."

"Trilby?" Corey said.

The blue-haired girl appeared on the screen, standing on a subway platform and looking very solemn. "I saw it happening as the train was pulling in. This creep, he—he had a knife . . . he was approaching this, like, little girl on the way home from school . . ." Her voice caught and she took a breath.

"*Little girl?*" Zenobia hopped up from the sofa. "I'm a high school senior!"

Mutti laughed softly. "Hoo, hoo, hoo."

"Well, that girl is like twenty," Corey said. "To her, you looked—"

"So . . . so . . ." On the screen, Trilby was in close-up, choking back tears. "So I guess I didn't care about the danger to me. I didn't even think. There was a fight. Everything happened so fast. I pulled the guy off to let her escape. And he lost his balance and f-f-fell on his knife."

"Whaaat? She's taking all the credit!" Zenobia shouted at the TV. "Corey's the one who saved me!"

"*Sssshhhh.*" Papou turned up the volume as Carla Hasty appeared on the screen again. "The attacker, who has not yet been identified, is reported in good condition at Saint Luke's Hospital with minor lacerations.

He is also reported to be wanted in connection with a string of robberies on the Upper West Side. . . ."

"Corey's a hero, Mutti," Corey's mom whispered.

"Like Stanislaw . . ." Mutti muttered.

"Like who?" Corey asked, but no one was paying attention.

"The real story will come out," Yiayia said, "when Zenobia presses charges."

Corey let out a sigh of relief and flopped back on the sofa. "Well, I'm glad the guy didn't die."

"Yeah, me, too, so I can nail his butt in the courtroom." Zenobia leaned down and cupped the back of Corey's head in her hand. "I'm glad *you* didn't die. You are my hero, little bro. I will never ever ever say a bad thing to you again." She gave Corey a hug and then kissed her grandparents one by one. "Papou, Yiayia, Mutti, 'bye, gotta do homework!"

As she ran out of the room, Mutti was calling out names now, in a world of her own. Corey's mom quietly wheeled her away, just behind Zenobia.

As a commercial started, Yiayia sat back down and sighed. "I still can't believe what happened, Corey. What are the chances you'd be waiting for an uptown train at the exact moment your sister arrived?"

"It's like you planned it," said Papou.

Corey gave the old man a glance. Papou's left eyebrow was raised sky-high. The message was clear:

We need to talk.

The park's stone wall was amber gray in the setting sun, as Corey and his grandfather crossed Central Park West. Neither of them said a word. It was a freakishly warm December evening, but Corey zipped his jacket tight. The temperature always seemed to drop the moment they reached the park side of the street.

"So, let me guess," Papou said. "You hopped, because something bad happened to your sister?"

Corey had to remind himself that Papou didn't know exactly what had happened. Changing the past meant that everything was reset, including people's memories. In Papou's mind, the robbery and the hospital trip never occurred. But Papou was a time traveler, too. Even though he still had a memory like any other human being, he knew something was up.

Corey had inherited the ability to time-hop from his papou, and they kept no secrets. "Yeah," Corey said. "I did."

Papou stopped at the entrance at Ninety-Sixth Street, next to the large stone slab in the wall carved "Gate of

All Saints." His face was lined and dark in the waning sunlight. Their neighbor Walter was approaching with Bailey, who was straining at the leash. "Hi there, we're late," said Walter as he passed. "Don't know if he's walking me or I'm walking him!"

"Hi, Baileeeeeeeey!" Corey shouted. But Bailey ignored him. It was as if he'd remembered Corey's snub from earlier by the subway stairs.

Normally Papou would say hi to Walter and crack some lame joke. But his eyes were fixed on Corey. "Was Zenobia badly hurt? Disfigured?"

"No, you saw her," Corey said.

"I mean, *before*," Papou said. "Was that the reason you hopped—she was terribly injured?"

"No," Corey replied.

"So . . . concussion? Great loss of blood?"

"I don't think so. She was upset. Mom wanted her to go to the hospital, you know, to rule out anything."

"Okay. So help me understand the *before* part, *paithi mou*," Papou said. "You went along with your mom to the hospital, and from there you ducked out in order to sneak back into the past and confront this knife wielder yourself? You decided to go it alone, putting your life at risk—even though your sister was shaken up and could have dealt with it the way people in New

13

York deal with things like this?"

Corey didn't like this line of questioning. It was so matter-of-fact. A scolding. It wasn't like Papou at all. "She's your granddaughter! If you could do what I can do, wouldn't you—"

"Ah, there's my point, Corey," Papou said. "We've talked about this, yes?"

"I know, I know," Corey said. "Along with the powers of being a Throwback comes great responsibility."

"Were you being responsible?" Papou asked. "What if you'd died? Who would go into the past to save you?"

Corey turned away. He knew the answer to that.

No one.

Papou could time-hop. Corey's best friend, Leila, could, too. The Upper West Side of New York City was headquarters to a group of time travelers called the Knickerbockers, and they were part of a bigger international group. But the rules of time applied to them all. The past was the past. It could not be changed. Period. No matter how many attempts you made, nature interfered. It stopped you in your tracks. You could jump on the back of John Wilkes Booth and he would still shoot Lincoln. You could try to poison Christopher Columbus, but he would still set sail. Corey's grandmother had died in the World Trade Towers on 9/11, and Papou himself had tried many times to rescue her. Each time he failed and failed again.

The idea of a Throwback, a real, honest-to-goodness history changer, had been a legend among the Knickerbockers. A tall tale.

It took Corey to make it real. He had saved his grandmother. But it wasn't easy. It took a failed try and a slip back into 1917. And Corey came close to dying there.

"Come with me," Papou said. "There's one more thing."

As he turned into the park, Corey asked, "Where are we going?"

"Into the North Woods," Papou said. "For a little refresher talk with a friend."

Which meant, Corey suspected, that they were going to see the mutant talking warthog formerly known as Cosmo deSmiglia. Who smelled something like a fart in a bed of rotten cheese.

"Oh. Come on." Corey stopped walking, forcing his grandfather to stop. "Smig? Why?"

Papou turned. "You need this. He will talk sense into your head. About ELSTTS."

"Else?"

"E-L-S-T-T-S," Papou spelled out. "Excessive life span time travel syndrome."

This was the flip side of time travel. It was dangerous to go back to a time when you were already alive. It seemed nature didn't like when two of you existed at the same time. Your body's genes, in Papou's scientific analysis, "freak out." They don't know how to handle it, something like magnetic poles repelling each other. With each visit, the agitation gets worse, until finally the body revolts. The genes shift and become something else. Something as far from human as possible.

Like Smig.

"Look, I promise, Papou, I'm not like Smig," Corey pleaded.

"Addiction to time travel is what caused him to be the way he is."

"I won't get addicted. I'm different."

The screech of tires made him stop in his tracks.

And a loud, unearthly scream.

By the time Corey spun around to see what happened, Walter Preston was crouched on the road. A set of black tire tracks led past him to an Uber cab, stopped at a slant halfway onto the grass.

"Oh, *Panayia* . . ." Papou muttered. He gathered his thumb and first two fingers into the Greek sign of the cross as he stepped closer—touching forehead, chest, right shoulder, heart.

Corey ran closer. Walter was shuddering, sobbing. The Uber driver had left his car and was running back toward the scene, his face creased with dismay. "I'm sorry," he said. "I'm so sorry. He just ran into the road. . . ."

As Walter stood, numb, other cars veered carefully around him. That was when Corey caught a glimpse of the inert figure on the road.

The beautiful Lab who had once been Bailey.

3

"Heyyy . . . Baileyyyy, what's u-u-u-up?" Corey shouted, racing up the stoop of the Prestons' brownstone. He was moving so fast, the dog almost jumped back through the front door.

The not-yet-dead dog. Because Corey was no longer in the present.

Calm down, he told himself. He willed his heart to stop banging in his chest. He had timed this one exactly right. This was a true microhop.

Ten minutes into the past. Time enough to save Bailey's life.

He still wasn't sure how he was able to do this. Somehow it worked through a metal artifact. A belt buckle from 1862, a subway token from 2001, the silver content of a photo from 1917—those were his first trips. But now he was able to slip hours and minutes, with nothing but coins from the present time. How?

It's like asking a control pitcher how to hit the corners of the strike zone, Papou had told him. *They just concentrate on doing it, and they do it.*

Sometimes it was best not to analyze.

"Oh, hi, Corey," said Walter Preston, closing the door behind him. "We're running late. Man, glad your sister's okay. I want to talk to you about what happened. Walk us to the park? Bailey really has to go—"

But Corey squatted at the landing by the front door, not letting Bailey get down the stoop, hugging him and scratching his belly. "I am so, so, so, so sorry I ran past you near the subway, big guy—you know I love you!"

Bailey whimpered and squirmed, his eyes darting nervously to the sidewalk. But Corey knew exactly where to scratch him and how much he liked it, and he soon gave in, licking Corey's face.

"Come on, Bails," Walter said. "Let's get you to the park before you pee on Corey." He gathered Bailey's leash, but Corey held tight.

Out of the corner of his eye, a half a block farther down Ninety-Fifth Street, Corey spotted the door to his brownstone opening. Through the front door walked Papou and . . . Corey.

Himself.

His body shivered, head to toe. Bailey hadn't yet seen the other Corey and neither had Walter. This was good. Seeing two Coreys would freak Walter out. Corey angled Bailey the opposite direction, toward Columbus Avenue, forcing Walter to turn his back to the Fletchers' brownstone.

Corey's body tingled. He felt weirdly cold. Was this a sign of ELSTTS? *Like magnets repelling,* Papou had said.

He blocked all that out. Bailey was whimpering like crazy, dying to get to the park. But Corey didn't care. He would take a blast of pee, full in the chest, to keep Bailey from harm.

Finally, with a painful, high-pitched yowl, Bailey jumped loose and leaped down the steps. "No-o-o-o!" Corey shouted.

The dog stopped at the curb, lifting his leg against a scraggly tree with a sign that read Please Do Not Let Your Dog Urinate Here.

"Awwwww, Bails, what are you doing?" Walter burst out laughing.

"Sorry," Corey said, trying to hide his feeling of relief.

"The irony is, I put that sign there," Walter said with a shrug. "Ah well, best-laid plans . . ."

As they waited for Bailey to do his business, Corey gave a sidelong glance up the block. His other Corey-self and Papou were disappearing around the corner of Central Park West. Slowly he stood. The delay had worked. Now he had to get out of sight, back to the time he'd just left.

"Well, I guess I better . . . um, do my homework," Corey announced.

Accompanying Walter and Bailey up 95th Street, he kept a deliberately slow pace. He said good-bye to them in front of his own building and watched intently as Walter and Bailey continued toward Central Park West.

He spotted the Uber speeding up the avenue. It would get to the intersection way before Walter. It would turn into the park without coming near Bailey.

Corey exhaled deeply. Time to return to the present. He reached into his pocket, grabbed a fistful of very warm coins, and closed his eyes.

His head felt like it would explode. He gulped air. His heart raced. For sure he had learned to pinpoint his trips better, but they still hurt. He blinked once, twice, until the familiar corner scene reappeared.

He was at the Gate of All Saints. The exact spot he'd left, where the cab had hit Bailey. He was the one and only Corey again, back in his "present" body. He was shoulder to shoulder with Papou, just as he'd been before the time hop. No one seemed to have noticed anything weird had happened.

Where was Bailey?

He stopped and spun around. His grandfather continued walking toward the tennis courts, lost in his own thoughts.

There. The Uber cab had driven past Corey. It was now disappearing between the stone walls of the transverse road, heading toward the East Side. Corey's eyes swept left, back toward the park entrance, then back over the wall. He scanned the area from 96th to 95th Street. There was Walter, visible over the park wall from the waist up. He was walking slowly up Central Park West, yanking on Bailey's leash. He hadn't reached the park yet.

He'd been delayed by Corey. And now everybody was safe and happy.

Corey wanted to whoop with joy. But it would weird out Walter to see him here. After all, Walter had just said good-bye to Corey back on 95th Street.

So instead Corey pumped his fist silently and ran

after Papou. The old man had reached the park's West Drive and was waiting while bike traffic cleared. Corey pulled him across the drive and onto a tree-lined path. "I saved a life, Papou," he blurted out.

"You what?" Papou stopped, glaring at Corey.

"Don't get mad at me. It was Bailey. He died. He was run over. You saw it. I saw it. So I went back and brought him back to life!"

"Just now? While we were walking?" Papou said.

"It was so . . . *easy*," Corey said. "Is that normal? I mean, it didn't used to be easy. When I tried to save Yiayia, I messed up everything. And now, all I do is hold the coins. They get warm, I think about what time I want to go to, and bam! It's like I went straight from crawling to tap dancing! I wanted to go back ten minutes, and I hit it. Ten exactly. Is it that easy for you?"

"No." Papou's face was creased with concern. "But I'm not a Throwback. I gave up time traveling long ago—"

"I know, I know, you're going to yell at me."

"Not yell, *paithaki*, but this just proves my point about getting addicted to traveling in time—"

"I couldn't just let Bailey die! You told me I had to be responsible."

"There are unintended consequences of changing

the past. You know this!"

"Right. That's what you say. That's what books and movies say. The butterfly effect. If you step on a butterfly in the past, the future falls apart. Chains and chains of events. When you come back to the present, Nazis are in power . . . or whatever," Corey said. "But so far all I've done is make *good* things happen. So isn't it responsible to do good things? To save lives? You were so sad before I saved Yiayia on 9/11. My whole life, I knew you were sad. You even looked different. Skinny, hunched over. Everything about you was different. But when I came back, it all shifted. You never lost her. You never knew that awful feeling!"

"I will of course always be grateful, Corey," Papou said. "I can't even imagine how I'd feel if she weren't here. But with all respect, you didn't save her. Not directly. What happened was a mistake, am I right? Something you did in nineteen seventeen—"

"Changed one small thing, I know—"

"Which accidentally saved her life many years later."

"But think about it—if that's what I did by accident, what about the stuff I can do on purpose?" Corey asked. "I'm better at it now. I can pinpoint my time hops almost to the minute. I saved a life, Papou. You should have seen Walter's face when Bailey was killed."

"I can only imagine."

"I don't know how I improved. Practice, I guess."

"Practice." Papou nodded. "Yes, the more you do it, the better you get. And the more eager to continue."

Silently he began walking north along the old bridle path. He seemed deep in thought, and Corey kept quiet. They climbed a gentle hill that bridged the transverse road. Below them, cars whizzed east and west. On the other side of the bridge, as they descended toward the North Meadow baseball fields, the old man finally spoke again.

"When I was a boy, I read Superman comics," he said. "Your great-grandparents wanted me to read the classics! But to me, comics were like the Greek myths— battles for the soul of humanity, good versus evil, the interplay between superpowers and mortals. Oh, I wanted superpowers to be real. I had a big fantasy life like you do. But I knew it was fantasy—until I began time-hopping. At first I didn't believe I was doing it. I thought it was my imagination. I began to think I was seriously mentally ill. It scared me, *paithi mou*. I didn't have anyone like me to explain it."

"But . . . but you must have inherited the ability from someone in the family, right?" Corey asked.

"Yes . . ." Papou looked out over the ball fields, but his eyes were somewhere else. "One night I had what I thought was a dream. I found myself on a dirt road in a small town in Greece. The full moon was the only light. I heard a high, painful shrieking. It came from a building in a field. It was painted completely white. There were bars on the window. A guard with a wooden club sat in front, but he was slumped on a chair, fast asleep. At first I thought it was some kind of prison. But the shrieking was mixed with cackling, laughing, nonsense words. And I knew what this building really was—an asylum. I crept closer, until a face suddenly appeared in the window. It was an old lady. She had no teeth. Her hair was like loose wires! I jumped. But she just smiled like she was expecting me. And she said, 'O Kostas, o levendis! Ella tha filaki to yiayia.'"

"What does that mean?" Corey asked.

"'Kostas, the brave one! Come kiss your grandmother.'"

Corey stopped short, and Papou turned to face him.

"Here's the thing, Corey," the old man continued. "I had heard about her. My family called her trellos—crazy. When they spoke of her, they invoked the evil eye." He raised his gnarled index and middle fingers into a V-sign and pantomimed spitting through them.

"Ptoo . . . ptoo . . . ptoo . . . always three times. I didn't know what to think. Was I crazy, too? If I admitted what I saw, would they laugh at me? Lock me up? So I said nothing. I retreated into stories, comics. Then I read one episode I never forgot. Superman makes the world rotate in the opposite direction. Why? To *reverse time*, so he can change a terrible tragedy in the past. This makes no sense, I know. But I began thinking. About superpowers. Maybe I did have one, and it was time travel. Hers, too! Maybe my *yiayia* and I were not crazy! I vowed to be like Clark Kent and Bruce Wayne, people trying to live a normal life while hiding a secret."

"Then I came along," Corey said.

"That's when I learned something new," Papou said. "What we do, all of us Knickerbockers, is not power. We go, observe, come back, that's all. We're like tourists in time. We can't change anything, no matter how hard we try. That's why people get addicted, like Smig. Like Leila's aunt Flora. You want to save a person. It should be so easy to do! But you fail and fail and fail. The frustration catches hold of you, the idea that if you try *one more time* . . . then you might succeed. You eventually give up. But that doesn't stop you. You keep going back anyway, for another reason—because it's the only way to be with that loved one. You go again and again.

27

Chances are good that you may meet yourself. You may meet many versions of yourself. And that is when you run into trouble. Eventually your body will punish you. Your genes somehow know that you shouldn't exist twice. They will force you to transspeciate. To become a creature that is as far from human as can be. Something hideous. And that is what concerns me."

"Papou, think about it," Corey said. "People keep going back because they fail to change things. Like you just said. But that's not me. I can succeed! So I won't need to keep going back, right? Which means I won't get addicted. And I won't transspeciate."

"I know human nature. You're a good boy, but success will make you bold. When you change one thing, you will want to change another. And another."

Corey fell silent. They were nearing the North Woods now. The trees were losing their color and gathering the darkness. "Just out of curiosity, Papou— how many time hops does it take to, you know . . . turn into a beast?"

Papou shrugged and took Corey's arm. "This, my boy," he said, "is why we're here. To find out."

4

Corey could smell Smig before seeing him. "Ucccch. Why would anybody come down here, ever?" he whispered.

"Usually he hides where no one can smell him," Papou explained. "But when he senses we're coming, he comes out of his cave."

"Lucky us."

They descended the path that led to a stream just below a waterfall. As they reached bottom, Corey heard a frantic rustling in the bushes.

"Smig?" Papou called out.

A scream broke the silence, followed by a low-pitched chuffing. A flash of white dashed through the underbrush from right to left, and Papou stopped in his tracks.

"That's not Smig," Corey said.

"Hello!" Papou shouted. "Who's down there?"

The white creature was out of sight. But now something was moving to the right, from the place where the white-furred creature had run. Under the waterfall, from the mouth of a small cave came a different animal, thick and grayish brown. Despite the darkness Corey could still make out two tusks, a ridge of spiked hair, and bloodshot eyes that seemed to glow with their own yellow light.

That was Smig.

"No one here but us chickens," came a husky, raw growl that was more grunt than voice. "I mean, chicken. Just me. I'm alone. Completely alone, minding my own business." He began making a weird, spitty, blowing noise.

"What are you doing?" Papou asked.

"Whistling an innocent tune," Smig said.

But Corey's eyes were trained on the bushes to his left, where he could see the white animal hiding. He had a suspicion what it was. Well, *who* it was. Flora was the time-traveling aunt of Corey's time-traveling best friend, Leila. Like Smig, Auntie Flora had time traveled too much for her DNA to withstand. She'd transspeciated into a creature that looked like a bright white cat on steroids, with a stout body like a badger and a snout like a dog. As a person, she'd been a Knickerbocker like Papou. Nowadays, she lurked around the Upper West Side, and the local kids had given her a different name.

Is that . . . Catsquatch? Papou mouthed.

Corey nodded.

What is she doing with Smig? Papou asked.

Corey shrugged. Picking up a branch, he crept closer and poked at the area. "Peekaboo . . ."

The white lump jumped. With a menacing *sssssss!* the creature known as Catsquatch leaped into sight, baring her teeth.

"Hello, Flora. We didn't expect to see you here," Papou said. He raised his eyebrows at Smig. "I hope we didn't . . . interrupt anything."

"Er, hrmmmmph, I can explain," Smig grumbled. "We are merely . . . colleagues, commiserating over our forlorn loves—er, *lives!*"

Papou sniffed. "Do I detect romance in the air?"

"That," Corey drawled, "is so disgusting."

"Ro—rom—? No, no, no, no, no!" Smig snuffled. "Don't be silly."

"Silly?" Now Catsquatch reared back on her haunches, glaring at Smig. "Do I embawwas you, Cosmo?"

Corey tried not to smile. Something about her animal jaw made it impossible for Auntie Flora, aka Catsquatch, to pronounced her r's. But it was important to be wespectful.

Respectful.

"Of course not, my dear!" Smig retorted. "It's merely a matter of . . . propriety."

If Smig weren't covered with thick bristles, Corey could swear he was blushing.

"What you love beasts do down here is none of our business," Papou said. "I've brought along Corey to discuss his future. To encourage him to take proper precautions. He has already time-hopped five times."

"Well . . ." Corey murmured. "More like seventeen."

"*Sevent—?*" Papou's eyes widened. "The Civil War soldier, the World Trade Center attack, New York in 1917, your sister on the subway, Bailey . . ."

"Remember when I got that perfect score on my

chemistry project?" Corey said. "And the time I told you to sell your Archer Street Corporation stock—"

"Ach, *Panayia mou!*" Papou quickly looked up to the heavens, then turned to Smig and Catsquatch. "You see? Talk some sense into my grandson, you two."

Catsquatch walked straight to Corey and stood on her hind legs again, placing her front paws on his shins. "My advice? Don't do it. I will not stand by and let my niece's boyfwiend become one of us!"

"I'm not her boyfriend," Corey murmured, feeling his face grow warm.

"Indeed, Flora, well said! Brava! You don't want this fate!" Smig snorted. A pungent aroma rose up from behind him, as if to emphasize the point.

"Guys, I'm a Throwback," Corey said. "I can change things. Maybe there's something I can do to turn you back into humans!"

"That *is* a tempting proposition," Smig remarked.

"Honey, so little is known about twansspeciation," Catsquatch said. "It's just too wisky."

"How much *is* known?" Corey pressed. "How many times does it take? And what happens if I only go back to long, long ago—like, *before* I was born? That way I wouldn't be in two places at the same time. My

DNA won't have anything to complain about. Does that protect me from transspeciation? Or is it just about the frequency?"

"He asks a lot of questions," Smig grunted.

"I'll stawt with question one," Catsquatch said. "It only took twelve times for me to twansspeciate."

"Oh?" Smig said. "It was two hundred forty-three for me . . . or maybe two hundred forty-four."

"*Whaaat?*" Corey said.

"Perhaps I was an outlier," the warthog snuffled. "I know a fellow who transspeciated after only three hops. He turned into a mosquito. Someone smacked him. What a waste."

"My deew fwiend, Pottsy Liscomb? She wacked up over a thousand hops and nothing happened," Catsquatch added. "But she was a mawathon wunner, vewy young and physically fit. She wetired fwom time-hopping at age twenty-nine, fully human. She has a vewy nice goblet from Ancient Wome. Also Awistotle's autogwaph."

"That's crazy!" Corey said. "That's not helpful at all! How am I supposed to know how many hops I can do?"

"You're a Throwback," Smig said. "Maybe you're immune. Maybe you can keep it going forever."

"I will not let him take that chance!" Papou shouted.

"Let's be calm and think this thwough, Gus," Catsquatch said. "Maybe we can weach a compwomise. He's young and stwong, like Pottsy. I think he just needs to keep twack of the wawning symptoms when he weturns into the pwesent from the past. A tingle in the body. A feeling of disconnection. A splitting headache."

"I get those already!" Corey said.

The park fell silent. Papou was giving Corey a dark, meaningful look.

"Well, they're not killer," Corey added. "But I feel them."

"Do you find yourself slipping in time, like, not coming back when you expect to?" Smig asked.

"That happens to us all," Catsquatch said. "Is haiw stawting to gwow on your cheeks and hands?"

"Do you have a sudden inexplicable urge to eat slugs?" Smig followed up.

"No, no, and heck no!" Corey shot back.

"Okay, some good signs," Catsquatch said.

Smig snorted. "I do not see this ending well. My boy, if I were a Throwback, I know what would happen. I'd be tempted never to stop. I'd go big. Prevent wars from happening. Encourage action against climate change. Prevent assassinations—"

"And how, pway tell, would you do this?" Catsquatch asked.

"I wouldn't," Smig replied. "And that's my point. Things would go wrong. I'd fail. I'd cause unexpected bad things to happen. I'd want to do it over again. Once you start, it is so hard to stop. You get caught in what the ancients call a chaos loop. A cycle of failure and escalating frustration. It sucks you in and you will never let go until . . . Well, my advice is, stop now while you can walk upright and smell fresh and sweet."

Papou smiled triumphantly. "You see?"

"Even a few times?" Corey asked. "What if I keep it up just until I feel symptoms?"

"If you must," Catsquatch said, "then my advice is, go big and go limited. Make a list of goals. And be vewy, vewy choosy."

"That," Papou said, his face sinking, "is not exactly the advice I wanted to hear."

He promised Papou he wouldn't do it.

He agreed at least five times that it was too risky.

But now, at 1:07 a.m., Corey's fingers flew across the keyboard as if someone had held a match to them.

He kept a history textbook open before him, and a bunch of Wikipedia pages on his screen.

Make a list. Go big. Change the world. It was so simple.

Limit himself. Keep it to a fixed number of time hops, and then—*slam*. No more. Door shut.

He could do it. At the first sign of transspeciation— one hair growing in the wrong place—he'd stop. He wasn't that dumb.

After a gazillion revisions, he sat back and looked at his work:

MY DREAM LIST

By Corey Fletcher

Possible Things to Prevent / Help / Change in History
THINK BIG!!!! HOLD NOTHING BACK!!!

Take AIDS drug info to drs	late 1970s/ early 80s
Expose 9/11 terrorists before attack	2001
Invest $1,000 in Microsoft, Apple, Amazon	1986, 1980, 1997
Stop Civil War	1860s
Stop World War I	1914
Stop World War II	1939

Stop Vietnam War	1960s
Buy cheap NYC brownstones (ask Papou for $$)	1900s?
Make peace Anglo settlers + Native Americans	1600s (?)
Stop Lincoln killer	1865
Warn Titanic	1912
Stow away on moon landing	1969
Expose climate change / bring green tech info	1900?
Tip off police to JFK killer	1963
Get Mets World Series tix, final game	1969, 1986
Stop cow from kicking lantern before Chicago fire	1871
Warn SF about earthquake	1906

Corey's eyes were bleary. He yawned, then shut his laptop. The list was overwhelming. And these were just some of the top ones in the history of the US. He would get to the other continents tomorrow.

Then he would have to narrow it down.

How many chances before he felt the symptoms? Before things went beyond headaches? He'd have to prioritize. The most important things first.

Chaos loop. A cycle of failure and escalating frustration.

It sounded horrible. But it wouldn't happen to Corey Fletcher. It couldn't. He was a Throwback.

The last thing he did before falling asleep was to touch his cheek. It was smooth, hairless, and human. And the thought of slugs did not make him hungry. Not one bit.

5

*B*onnnng . . . *bonnnng* . . .

Corey jumped out of bed, not knowing how he'd ended up there.

He recognized the chimes of the old clock on the living room mantel. But the last time he'd heard them was years ago. The chimes had been disabled.

Rubbing his eyes, he saw that his laptop was still open. He tried to waken the dark screen but nothing happened. It was completely shut down. After rebooting he discovered that his list—the complicated, long list—was gone.

He groaned. For a moment he suspected he'd time-hopped. But nothing had changed. One thing about time travel, you *knew* when it happened. You felt it.

There must have been a power outage. He would have to start over.

Bonnnng . . . bonnnng . . .

Four chimes. Four a.m. He staggered into the living room, yawning, and stared curiously at the old clock. It had been silent since he was a little boy. Back then, the chimes had spooked him, waking him every hour. He'd begged his mom to throw it out but instead she had somehow "fixed" it, silenced the chimes.

They weren't silent anymore.

Corey carefully swept aside some photos so he could examine the clock. On its base was an inscription: Luis Velez / New York Telephone Company Pioneer / 35 Years of Loyal Service.

He smiled. He only vaguely remembered his other grandfather, his mom's dad. Papi Luis had died when Corey was four.

Carefully Corey swiveled the clock around. On the back was a panel with a small hook. He turned it and pulled, and the panel swung open to reveal brass gears attached to three tiny hammers. The hammers were precisely poised over metal chimes, but now Corey could see that Mom had stuffed a wad of cotton between them, jamming and silencing the hammers.

By now the cotton had disintegrated into dirty

white flecks. The hammers, for the first time in years, were striking the chimes again.

"Sorry, sweetie," came his mom's voice from the living room entryway. With a grin, she held up a piece of fresh cotton.

"Awesome. All this time I never knew how you did that."

"Well, I figured my little hack wouldn't work forever." Mom quickly stuffed the new cotton into place. "You know, your *abuelo* was so proud of this clock. Truth be told, I think it's ugly. Mutti would tease him about it. 'Thirty-five years you give the company, and all you get is a lousy clock? How about a little house in Puerto Rico?' She was a character. So funny and full of life. They really adored each other."

As she shut the panel, Corey took her parents' framed wedding photo down from the mantel. In it, Corey's grandfather was laughing so hard his eyes were closed. He was dressed in his crisp World War II United States Army uniform, his dark eyebrows lifted way up, his teeth gleaming. Next to him, Corey's grandma was staring at the camera with mischievous, dancing eyes, her lips puckered as if to keep a straight face. "Look at them," his mom said. "They never could take a serious picture."

Corey thought about his grandmother all shriveled and haunted looking in her wheelchair. "It's hard to imagine her like that now."

"She had a tough life. I think the joking covered up the pain. You've seen this one, right?" Mom put the wedding picture in its place and held up an even older photo. It was a family, looking very formal and posed—a bespectacled, balding man with a beard and waxed mustache; a hefty-looking, white-haired woman with a feathered hat; three scowling boys in shorts; and a thin, dark-haired, smiling little girl.

"Mutti's family?" Corey said. "She's the girl, right? In Poland?"

"Helga Meyer, before she became Helga Velez." His mom nodded. "She lost all of her family in Warsaw, when they were taken by the Nazis. She hid with a kind family, but they were poor and could not feed her well. Thin and weak, she was smuggled away by the Resistance, to a border town in Austria. From there they managed to smuggle her out of Europe entirely, to South America. That same day the Nazis ambushed the village, killing everyone. Blessedly Mutti was on her way to Brazil and then eventually to Puerto Rico. That's where she met Papi, where he was stationed in San Juan. It was love at first sight."

"Wow . . . she never talked about any of that," Corey said. "Except the part about meeting Papi."

"That part was happy," Mom said. "The rest was painful. She would talk about it to us once in a while, but she didn't want us to say anything. 'Let bygones be bygones,' she told us."

"What happened to them?" Corey asked. "Her family?"

With a heavy sigh, his mom placed the photo back on the mantel. "I don't know. I don't know if anyone does. There was one thing. . . ."

She disappeared for a moment, returning with a small, weathered cardboard box. Inside, on a small cotton bed, was a small, rectangular metal box. "A cigarette case," Mom said. "Look inside."

Corey unclasped the box and took out a battered identification card. It was brittle to the touch as Corey held it close to read.

"Stanislaw Meyer," Mom said. "Mutti's brother. Your great-uncle. They found this on his body in the woods, near the end of the war."

"The Nazis shot him?" Corey asked.

"Ironically, no," Mom replied. "In nineteen forty-five Stanislaw was part of a group being marched through the forest, to be taken to a labor camp. But the Nazi commander grew weary of the snow and cold. And so, when the prisoners stopped to rest, he and his men shot them all. Except for Stanislaw. He had had a sense something was wrong. And so he excused himself to pee. He went behind an abandoned hunting shack and hid. When he heard the shots, he stayed there. They had forgotten about him. They didn't care. They knew it was a shorter walk to go back to Nazi headquarters than to reach the camp. So Uncle Stanislaw waited until the Nazis were gone. And then he ran."

Mom gently took the ID card and placed it back in the box. Her eyes were watering.

"So . . . how did he die?" Corey asked.

"Somehow he made it through the forest," Mom continued. "He saw the lights of some town or city. But just before he made his way through to civilization, he found the body of an armed Nazi soldier hidden in the bushes. To be safe, he took the man's pistol. Moments later he saw a convoy of Nazi vehicles approaching on the road. He could see they saw him. So in panic, he shot at them. They . . . they shot back. . . ."

"The Nazis killed him?" Corey said. "After all that?"

"It wasn't even Nazis. The convoy was *captured vehicles*, Corey. Resistance fighters were driving them. Stanislaw was killed . . . by the people who would have rescued him. Because of a hurried mistake. His story would have been lost had he not managed to tell them who he was before he died."

"What a waste," Corey said. He took the box and held it. "Can I keep this?"

"But this is such a ghoulish, sad thing, Corey." Mom cupped her hand around the back of his neck. "I've put such sad thoughts in your head, you'll never sleep."

"I'll be okay, I'm just proud of how brave he was," Corey said. "Night, Mom. Thanks."

As he got to his room, he looked at his laptop's screen. He thought about his lost list of potential historical events to change.

Maybe he didn't have to reconstruct it now.

He couldn't stop thinking about his great-uncle and great-grandparents. He tried to memorize their features. He sat down and started to research them as best he could. He searched on their names. He looked for their faces in images of families being marched out of their homes at gunpoint. He looked for them in photos of death camp prisoners. But he came up empty-handed everywhere. It was as if they never existed.

He plunged deeper and read about the millions of Jews slaughtered for no reason, completely erased from the record of humanity. He read about the Poles and gay people and anyone the Nazis decided were expendable. He dug into reports of "experiments" by Nazi doctors, who injected diseases into people and forced them to die in slow agony. He saw the photos of mass graves and starved, zombielike prisoners.

As the sun's rays began to blush the morning air, Corey was watching a film called Triumph of the Will. Much of it was archival footage of Adolf Hitler addressing a crowd that seemed to stretch to the horizon. But the dictator's voice was tinny, nasal, and squeaky. He pounded his fists like a toddler and jerked his head as he barked, which sent greasy hair flying across his forehead. It made Corey laugh. He couldn't help thinking that the people in the crowd must have been laughing, too. But when the camera cut to them, they didn't look snarky or embarrassed. Their faces were adoring, smiling, enthusiastic. Some cried with joy.

It was a sea of love for a man who promised a "pure"

society, a future cleansed of anyone he didn't like.

For example, Mutti's family.

Corey's family.

He shut the laptop, feeling sick. Hitler had followed through. Those adoring faces had allowed the murders. Some had supplied the chambers with poison gas and pulled the triggers of rifles. They had gone along with the extermination of human beings as if they were insects. Millions of lives into nothingness.

Not, not nothingness, Corey thought.

The past wasn't nothing.

As long as he was on this earth, the past was alive. A place he could go. A thing he could touch.

Going back didn't have to be about changing little things. Or things that were too big to contemplate. The decision didn't have to be so hard or involve lists.

An idea began forming in his head. And he knew he would not get to sleep at all.

6

"Don't say no."

It wasn't the usual greeting Corey gave Leila Sharp when they had breakfast at the Mila Café on Columbus Avenue. But Corey hadn't slept since the clock chimed, and it was already after 9:00. He wasn't in the mood for chitchat.

Already the place was nearly full. She sipped from a cup of hot chocolate as she sat, giving him a baffled look. "Uh, good morning to you, too. I don't know what I'm not supposed to say no to. But before you start getting all weird on me, I wanted to apologize."

"For what?"

"For asking you to help me with my German vocabulary flash cards yesterday, just after you'd nearly

49

died rescuing your sister. I didn't know that until later."

"Oh, right. You're welcome," Corey said. "I mean, thank you. She got hurt, so I had to go back and correct that."

Leila cocked her head. "Wait. That was a time hop?"

"Yup." Corey sat forward so he could speak softly. Being a time-hopper too, Leila was the only one he could talk to besides Papou, Catsquatch, and Smig. "And then I did another one, to save Bailey's life."

"Two in the same day?"

Corey could see the disapproval on her face. Leila was so easy to read. "Well . . . yeah. I saw my sister get beat up. I saw Bailey die. You're welcome. Think about what would have happened if I'd done nothing. I mean, what would you do if you were in my shoes?"

"Okay, I get that," Leila said. "It's great that you did those things. But I have a creepy feeling about this. I can't help it. My aunt Flora's life was ruined because—"

"I know! I spoke to her about this. And also to Smig." Corey lowered his voice another notch. "Oh. Did you know they're having a . . . thing?"

"What kind of thing?"

"They're going out."

Leila's lip curled into a sneer. "I just lost my appetite."

"Anyway, transspeciation doesn't have any rules, really," Corey said. "It's not like I'm allowed ten more times and then, *bam*, Corey-Beast! I mean, it *could* be ten times, or three. It could also be hundreds. But the thing is, there are warning signs. Hair growing in weird places, you feel a sudden taste for gross things . . ."

Leila peered into Corey's hot chocolate cup. "You're not drinking prune juice, are you?"

"Ha ha. Not yet," Corey said.

"But at some point, when you feel those weird things happen, you'll have to stop," Leila said. "Right?"

"Exactly. So what if I'm one of the people who only has a few times, Leila? I can't stop thinking about that. I don't want to waste my gift. I don't want to spend the rest of my life wondering if I did everything I could have done. So at about five in the morning I came up with this new plan."

"No," Leila snapped.

"I told you not to say that. Give me a chance—"

"Corey, I know you," Leila said. "You're going to ask me if you should travel in time and do something really, really stupid." Leila sipped her hot cocoa, which didn't look hot anymore. "Maybe you need to go back to sleep. It's Saturday. No diss, but you look terrible."

Corey broke off a chunk of chocolate chip muffin

but he wasn't feeling very hungry. He told her all the details about the night—his insomnia, the clock, the photos of his grandmother's family, his mom's story about the Nazi abduction and his grandparents' romance, the creepy Hitler footage. . . .

Leila listened patiently. "I didn't know the part about your grandma meeting your grandpa. It's so romantic."

"Not if you think about the reason she had to leave her country," Corey said. "Watching her whole family be taken away to die. How could she have lived with that? I mean, when I was a kid, she was always smiling and laughing. But now her dementia is getting worse. She calls out for her dad and mom, and her brothers, Jakub, Stanislaw, and Aleksander. Sometimes she screams in English, sometimes in Polish, sometimes Spanish. It's like she saved up the pain over her whole life, and now her brain won't let her hide it anymore. Like she's facing down a monster."

Leila sighed and looked out the window. "My grandfather was like that. When Opa Joseph got old, he screamed at his caregivers, warning them about the Nazis. But it was all in German and I had to translate. Did you know his name was Josef Scharfstein, and he changed it to Joseph Sharp at Ellis Island? He lost his mother and two older brothers. One was a doctor and the other was a concert pianist."

"You get this, Leila. You understand. Your grandpa, my mutti, they swallowed all their bad memories. It was like slow poison. There were so many families like that. All those millions of lives erased—inventors, musicians, writers, doctors. Imagine how much better the world would be if they didn't die!"

He let his words hang in the air. Leila eyed him carefully. "What are you saying, Corey?"

"You're going to tell me I'm crazy, and maybe I am," Corey said. "But just listen. I brought my grand-mother back from the dead. I saved the life of a Civil War soldier. I kept my sister from being mugged. I res-cued Bailey. Every time I've tried to change something in the past, it's been for a good reason, and it worked. But it's been for me, Leila, or for someone close to me. And that's just not fair. I can do so much more. If you have only a limited number of times you can change the past, and you're the only one who can do it—why not go big?"

"Corey's there's big and there's biiiiig. You're going to go back and single-handedly defeat the Nazis? Is that it?"

Corey took a deep breath. "Well, yeah, that's sort of the idea, but—"

"*Do you know how insane that sounds?* Who do you think you are, Corey Fletcher—a superhero?"

"Superman could fly," Corey said. "Spider-Man could climb with his web. Thor had his hammer. What do *you* call what I have? What do you call being a Throwback?"

Leila stared at him, frozen, for a good minute. Then she stood and lifted her cup from the table. "Well, I guess if you're SuperCorey, you don't need me. You can do everything yourself—"

Corey took her arm gently. "Leila, you can travel in time. I can change time. You're fluent in German. I'm not. What if you and I went back together?"

"To when?" Leila said. "And to do what? Drop a bomb on Germany?"

"That's silly."

"Assassinate Hitler?"

"Well . . ."

"No. No. And *no!*" Leila pounded the table, nearly spilling Corey's hot chocolate. "I can't believe you're thinking this. We're just kids!"

"We wouldn't do the assassination ourselves," Corey said. "I did research. There *was* an attempt. And it was foiled. Maybe we could just . . . unfoil it."

"That would make us accessories to murder," Leila said. "And in case you were absent that day in Sunday school, it's morally wrong to kill."

"It's morally right to allow a guy to butcher as many people as the entire population of New York City—including your ancestors and mine? It's right to allow it when there's a chance you can prevent it?"

"No!"

"So you'll do it?"

"No!" Leila turned toward the door. "This is crazy. This is out there. This is absolutely bonkers. Did you even think what would happen if you stopped Hitler? Your grandmother would never be smuggled to South America, and she'd never meet your grandfather, right? So you wouldn't exist!"

"But I *do* exist!" Corey pointed out.

"Everything adjusts when you change the past, right?" Leila said. "So wouldn't you adjust your own self out of existence?"

"Then how could I change the past if I never existed?"

"I don't know! Do I look like Einstein? How can we figure that out unless it actually happens?"

"Exactly!" Corey said. "Look, first we get Hitler. If

we can do that, how hard can anything else be? We make it a project to get Mutti and Papi to meet. That would be the easy part."

"Easy? You are making me cry, Corey Fletcher."

"So . . . we just let eleven million people die . . ." Corey said, his heart dropping.

"I—how can I answer that?" Leila swallowed and turned away.

"Just say yes," Corey insisted.

Leila pulled open the door and turned back toward Corey. "Give me twelve hours. I'll have an answer for you then."

As she left, three or four pigeons flew away from the front of the door. Corey felt no desire to eat them. His appetite was just fine. Normal as can be.

He smiled and finished his chocolate chip muffin.

7

Leila paced her bedroom.

Corey's plan was absolutely nuts.

She kept trying to think her way around this. To give him the benefit of the doubt. But no matter how she looked at it, his idea was more like a sci-fi movie trailer: *When two brave thirteen-year-old time travelers find themselves face-to-face with history's greatest evil, anything can happen . . . and does!* His scheme was well-meaning. Like Corey, it had heart. Huge heart.

But it was insane.

She had to tell Corey no, and she had to do it now. That would stop the whole thing. What did he plan to do, bring back a gun and shoot Hitler? How would he get close enough? How would a thirteen-year-old kid with no knowledge of German even figure out how to get to Hitler? Without her language skills, there wasn't much he could do in Germany. If he knew he had to do this on his own, he would come to his senses.

For the tenth time that morning, she picked up her phone.

Flopping onto her bed, she typed NO in a text to Corey. As she poised her thumb over Send, she stopped. Her eye fixed on the pile of boxes by her bedroom door—all Auntie Flora's stuff.

Leila's mom had agreed to take it, not long after Flora "left" Uncle Lazslo. The poor guy couldn't understand why his wife had done that. He thought they'd been getting along just fine. And in truth, they had been. But Flora had never told him about her time-hopping. Or about transspeciation.

It was only a few boxes. Someday she'd ask Auntie Flora what to do with it, but for now Leila didn't mind looking after it. Leila's mom kept referring to it as "old junk," but it wasn't junk, really. It contained all Flora's secrets. Including the artifact that took Leila into the past for the first time.

Sometime earlier today, her mom had tidied it all up. Now the boxes were stacked neatly. Each one had a label, in Uncle Laszlo's precise, engineer's handwriting.

Leila's eyes were drawn to a big one on top, one she hadn't yet touched:

SCHRFSTN
FML MMRBL
☹ ☹ ☹

Scharfstein. Uncle Laszlo thought it was efficient to leave out vowels.

It took her a moment to figure out the other two words: *Family Memorabilia.* This must have been Auntie Flora's collection of old stuff. She was born Flora Scharfstein—Opa Joseph's only daughter.

The frowny faces scared Leila a little. The family history was tragic, so who knew what was inside?

The box was about two feet high. She picked it up and heard a dull, musical sound. Setting the box down, she yanked open the top. The yellowing tape quickly gave way.

Inside, at the top of a pile of sheet music, was a tiny red toy piano. As Leila picked it up, it slipped out of her hand and fell to the floor with a loud clatter. White veneers fell off three or four keys. Next to them landed a tarnished brass medal on a faded ribbon.

She lifted the piano and held it to the light.

"Wow . . ."

It was sturdy, made of wood, and on the back was a carved relief of some somber-faced musician with curly hair, maybe Beethoven or Mozart. A label fell off the piano's side, its adhesive tape brown and brittle. It fell to the floor, its label side up.

1895. Das kleine Fritzchens erstes Klavier!

Little Fritzie's first piano.

She heard a soft rap at the door, and her mom entered. "Is everything okay? I made us some . . ." Her voice drifted off as she saw the open box and the piano. "What on earth is that?"

"Mom, who was Fritzie?" Leila asked, handing her the piano.

Her mom examined it gingerly, as if it were made of crystal. She picked up the ribboned medal from the floor and placed that gently on top. "He was your great-grandfather. Opa's dad. A trained concert pianist. Everyone said he was so passionate, he could make you cry. 'A better player than Horowitz!' Opa always said."

"Who?"

"Vladimir Horowitz may have been the best concert pianist of his time. I think Opa was exaggerating."

"Was Great-grandpa Fritzie famous?" Leila asked.

Leila's mom shook her head. She held the piano to

the light, her eyes moistening. "It was rough for artists and musicians in Poland, even before the war, so he ran a textile business to support his family. But he played professionally from time to time. Until the day the Nazis took him from a concert hall in Leipzig. Just ripped him from his seat in the middle of a rehearsal. They didn't even let him finish or pack a bag. They accused him of playing decadent music. Whatever that meant."

Leila's breath caught in her throat. She glanced down at the box. At the top was a decaying book titled *Bach Chorále*. And resting on it was a folded photograph, facedown.

As she turned it over, she and her mom gasped.

It was an image of a beaming man, sitting with his hands poised over a piano keyboard. On his chest he wore a small, crude-looking cloth Star of David with the word JUDE printed inside. Behind him, beaming even more, were a teenage girl, two teenage boys, and a younger boy. With a mischievous smile, the younger boy was proudly planting a kiss on the pianist's cheek.

Even with his lips pursed, Leila could tell the little guy was Opa Joseph.

"Oh dear . . ." Leila's mom said. "They all look so much like your father. . . ."

Leila opened her mouth to speak, but no words came out. She could not stop looking at the word JUDE.

It meant *Jew*.

In the eyes of the Nazis, it marked you with shame. It meant you were barely more than an animal. It allowed the Nazis to destroy your life if they so pleased.

As her mom left, Corey's words came back to Leila.

Inventors, musicians, writers, doctors. Imagine how much better the world would be if they didn't die. . . .

She looked at her text. It hadn't been sent yet, so she deleted it. She took a good two minutes trying to compose what she wanted to say.

Finally she typed out two words:

I'm in.

8

The first thing Corey noticed in the Sharps' apartment was an echo of muffled, scratchy classical music, like a piano trapped in a tin can.

As he walked past Leila's mom's room, he could see her through the open door. She was listening to a vinyl record on a turntable, her eyes closed as she swayed to the tune. He followed Leila down the long hallway into her bedroom. Her pillows were covered with old photos, in and out of frames. Sheet music lay neatly arranged in a checkerboard on her bed, around a toy piano. Ticket stubs, trinkets, jewelry, notebooks, silverware, and broken statuettes were strewn about her floor. "I think we have some good artifacts," she said.

"I don't know where you're going to put your back-pack, though."

"I'll keep it on," Corey said.

He ran his fingers along the piano. It was sturdy, made of wood and steel. He picked up a faded medal Leila had draped over the top. It was still attached to a shredded ribbon. "'Frederick Scharfstein, *Erster Preis*,'" Corey read slowly. "Does that mean 'first prize'?"

"Yup," Leila said. "Frederick was my great-grand-father Fritzie's full name. The music coming from Mom's room? That's Fritzie playing Bach. They recorded him a few months before he was killed. If you listen closely, you can hear his voice. Just a hint of a soft 'uh . . . uh . . . uh' in rhythm. He did that, kind of qui-etly grunted along with the music."

Corey stepped back into the hallway. The piano was really racing now, the notes spilling out fast and furious. Through the hisses and crackles of the old recording, Corey could hear a human voice humming along, low and soft. It gave him a chill. "That's actually him."

"The family managed to hide away some record-ings," Leila said, "and all this other stuff. I'm not sure how they did it."

"Or *why*," Corey said. Much of the artwork was

crude, street scenes with buildings that slanted the wrong way, portraits with crooked eyes and weird smiles, animals that seemed to be floating above the pastures. "Most of the art is pretty ugly."

"It's got to be, like, refrigerator art. The parents saving the kids' masterpieces."

Corey held up a metal-framed drawing of a horse in a field, not much bigger than a cell phone. At the bottom it was signed FS 1908. "Or their own."

"FS—Frederick Scharfstein," Leila said. Her face brightened as she ran her fingers along the metal frame. "Corey, this is amazing. This could take us back!"

"What would we do in Poland in nineteen-oh-eight?"

"Not Poland—*Vienna*," Leila said. "Opa's family traveled a lot. That's why he knew so many languages. They were living in Berlin when Fritzie was old enough for high school. Back then, if you had some money and your kid was an artistic genius, you packed that kid off to Vienna, in Austria. It was really the center of culture in Europe. Fritzie dreamed of becoming an artist. His parents, my great-greats, knew Fritzie's greatest gift was music, so they sent him to a place where he could study both. Vienna had a famous music conservatory and an academy of fine arts."

"Okay, so how does this help us?" Corey said.

"Did you pay attention at all in World History class?" Leila said.

"No, I've been too busy changing it," Corey replied.

With an exasperated sigh, Leila pocketed the small framed photo and darted over to her desk. Her fingers flew over her laptop keyboard, and when she was done she turned the screen toward Corey. On it was a Wikipedia entry adorned with the brooding, familiar face of Adolf Hitler.

"Hitler spent many years in Vienna, trying to be an artist," Leila pointed out as she scanned the piece. "Hitler was born in eighteen eighty-nine, Great-grandpa Fritzie in eighteen ninety. Many years later, Opa would shake his fist and say, 'If only we'd known what he would become, Papa could have poked his eyes out!'"

"Did they know each other?" Corey asked.

"I don't think so," Leila said.

"But they were studying in the same town, and that's good enough," Corey said. "Which means that if we go there, we could get to him before he became . . . Hitler Hitler."

"That's what I was thinking."

"Okay . . . we need a plan for this . . . we can't just hop into Vienna and smack him over the head with a big sausage." Corey began pacing the room. "Or maybe we could. It wouldn't leave a trace."

"Maybe we can do this without killing him," Leila said.

"But he's *Hitler!*" Corey protested.

Leila exhaled. "Okay. Close your eyes. Imagine you have a gun in your hand. Somehow, conveniently, you're face-to-face with Hitler."

"How?" Corey asked.

"I don't know, he comes out of the men's room— this is a thought experiment!" Leila said. "Now. There he is. Inches away. He smiles and says '*Guten Abend.*' Which means 'Good evening.'"

"What if it's morning?"

"*The point is* . . . do you see yourself lifting the gun and killing him? Even though he's Hitler? Are you capable of that? Or does your hand start to wobble? Do you have second thoughts? I mean, be truthful. Because if you don't shoot instantly, and even if you do, those Nazis are all over you. And that doesn't turn out well."

Corey nodded. She had a point. If they were going to meet Hitler as a student, maybe there was a way to defeat him with a more normal, non-killing plan. "Okay, he dreamed of being a famous artist, right? If he succeeded, maybe he wouldn't have become Dr. Evil.

What if we were able to nudge him in that direction?"

"How? Like, promote his paintings?"

"Yeah, that was a dumb idea."

"No! It's got potential." Leila began pacing, which in her room meant three steps forward and three steps back. "We could bring money into the past. We'd have to get hold of old-fashioned German currency—marks. We could buy up lots of his paintings. People will get the idea he's really popular. We'll drive up demand and maybe he'll actually become a famous artist and not need to go into politics."

"Unless," Corey said, "his stuff really sucks."

"It's not about quality, it's about popularity. We'll do a social media campaign, using . . . whatever they used. This could work, Corey."

"Really?" Corey said.

Leila fell silent. As the strains of Bach wafted through the door, Corey could read her mind. They wanted this thing to work, but it was really sketchy.

"We'll keep thinking," she said.

Corey scanned the debris in the room again. His eye went right to a twisted hunk of rusted metal, which looked like it had been chewed up by the Incredible Hulk. As he picked it up, an old envelope dangled from it on a string.

Carefully he reached into the envelope. Its edges disintegrated into flakes and dust as he pulled out an old photo, which had a handwritten message on the back.

The photo showed two older women standing at a gate marked with a sign in another language. They wore sunglasses and their white hair was done up in a sixties-style beehive. "Do you know who they are?" Corey asked.

"No clue," Leila replied.

Corey turned over the photo. On the other side was a handwritten message:

CLARA, MEIN LIEBCHEN:
VERGISS NICHT.
HÖR NICHT AUF ZU VERSUCHEN
11/39
—M. STROBEL

Leila came closer. "'Dear Clara'—the *chen* at the end is what you add when you like someone a lot—'Do not forget. Do not stop trying.' I don't know who M. Strobel is. I guess these are the two people in the photo."

"What wouldn't they want to forget?" Corey said. "It sounds ominous."

"November nineteen thirty-nine . . ." Leila was

already flipping through her phone. "It was a really bad year over there. It's when the Nazis started conquering Europe. We didn't enter the war until nineteen forty-one, but horrible things were happening."

Corey looked over her shoulder as she scrolled through a history of World War II. "Kristallnacht was November, but nineteen thirty-eight, a year earlier," Leila said. "When the Nazis destroyed Jewish shops, breaking glass and kidnapping people, forcing them to go to death camps. Maybe this was a one-year anniversary? This could be something left over from the destruction."

"Maybe we should go back to nineteen thirty-eight," Corey said.

"Like, just some random time in nineteen thirty-eight?" Leila asked. "Why?"

"To help out," Corey said. "If we get there, I can do some microhopping to get us back to *before* Kristallnacht. Then we can warn people, convince at least some of them to escape before it's too late."

"But . . . what about Hitler?" Leila asked.

"One step at a time," Corey said. "Maybe when we're there we can do some spying, meet some people in the Resistance. Time travelers make great spies, Leila. You and me, everyone in the twenty-first century, we know where Hitler went and what he did. We may have to snoop around in the past, then come back and do research so we can really nail a plan. But if we make friends with the right people, if we tip them off, they can do the dirty work."

"You really think that would work?" Leila asked.

Corey shrugged. "At least as well as trying to turn Hitler into Mona Lisa Guy."

"DaVinci," Leila said. But she didn't look convinced.

Corey knew if he hesitated, they'd never do anything. He held tight to the metal thing. It was beginning to feel warm. "Um, I'm needing an answer now, I think."

"Corey . . . ?" Leila said.

It didn't take long before he started to see white and feel like his own body was about to fly apart. "Hold on to me," he said.

"You're not actually doing this?" Leila said.

"Not by myself!"

"We haven't talked it through—"

"Hold on to me! Now!"

He felt Leila's fingers clasping his arm. He turned to face her, but all he saw was a field of white.

And all he heard was a sound like a jet engine.

9

When Corey came to, he was staring into the face of a dead chicken.

Gasping, he pushed it away and scrambled to his feet.

Leila was screaming.

"Sorry!" Corey said.

"What just happened?" Leila looked as woozy and confused as Corey felt.

The chicken, saying nothing, remained in a puddle on the muddy road. Next to it was Auntie Flora's twisted piece of metal, sending up wisps of smoke.

Not two feet away a woman stared at Corey and Leila, openmouthed. She was wearing a gray, old-timey raincoat and too much makeup. She clutched a paper bag full of groceries in one hand and a leaky umbrella in the other. It was raining pretty heavily, and water dripped from the edges of a thick kerchief she'd pulled around her head.

Corey caught a glimpse of a sign that said Rosenheimer Street. The road was lined with two- to four-story buildings, and just ahead was a grand archway marked Bürgerbräukeller. "Where the heck are we?" he whispered.

"I don't know," Leila said, her face darkening as she spotted the metal shard on the ground. "And I don't know why you just thought you could hop in time without even discussing it. Welcome to nineteen thirty-nine, I guess." Leila attempted a smile at the woman and said, *"Entschuldigen Sie, bitte."*

The woman eyed them head to toe with a baffled expression, as if they'd come dressed in Halloween costumes. Then she let loose a torrent of foreign words as she snatched the chicken out of the puddle.

"Is that German?" Corey asked.

"A weird dialect of it," Leila said. "I think she's calling you a chicken thief. I also think we shocked her. Considering, you know, we appeared out of nowhere from the future."

The woman had turned and was now heading

toward the archway. "WE . . . COME . . . IN . . . PEACE . . ." Corey called out.

"Shouting at her slowly is not going to make her understand English. Hang on, let me try again. I'll find out where we are." Leila ran after the woman, asking her a question in German.

Corey scooped up the piece of metal and shoved it in his backpack. He caught up with Leila and her new friend at the archway. His teeth were chattering, but he didn't know if it was from the cold, the rain, or the time travel. The woman had extended her umbrella to cover Leila but didn't seem concerned about Corey.

He followed them down a path to a massive brick building with the same name that adorned the archway—Bürgerbräukeller—over double wooden doors. The woman tried them, but they were locked. This caused another explosion of words, as she set down her bags and fumbled in her pocket for keys. "What's she saying?" Corey asked.

Leila stepped back and lowered her voice. "I'm not getting one hundred percent of it. But this is a major restaurant and she works here. We're in Munich, Germany, and her name is Maria."

Corey looked around. "Did you ask her what year it is?"

"Uh, no, that is not a normal question," Leila replied. "She is insisting that we come in and have breakfast. Someone was supposed to open the place this morning at six thirty, but he didn't show up. She thinks our clothing is weird, but when I told her we were Americans, that seemed to satisfy her. I said we were orphans visiting an uncle, and he's at work."

"That's so lame."

"She bought it. Anyway, to answer your question, the artifact said nineteen thirty-nine and that would make sense from the things she said. She mentioned Nazis. She also said that everyone is working around the clock and receiving less for it. Which would make sense for Germany before the war. She's very opinionated."

With an exasperated grunt, Maria pushed open the heavy wooden door. Corey caught a blast of pungent air, a combination of food spices, stale cigarette smoke, and spilled beer. But it was warmer and much drier inside, and that counted for something.

They stepped into a marble lobby with a carved wooden desk that contained an old-fashioned telephone with a brass bell and an open leather-bound ledger. But Maria immediately veered to the right, down a wide stone staircase.

It was dark, but Corey could see the outline of an

enormous underground space, nearly the size of a city block. At the bottom, Maria pressed a button on the wall. Above them, a matrix of six giant, elaborate chandeliers came to life across a vaulted ceiling. The light bathed a neat array of tables in a soft sepia glow. Chairs sat upside down on the tabletops, like wooden families frozen in place during a dinner. Balconies lined all four walls, containing sturdy railings and more tables. Under one of those balconies, along the opposite wall, was a stage with a podium.

"*Schön, ja?*" Maria said.

"Yes, beautiful," Leila replied. "Guess they have entertainment here. *Haben Sie Theaterstücke hier?*"

Maria nodded. "*Und Reden. Sie sind ganz berühmt.*"

"'And speeches,'" Leila translated. "'They're very famous.'"

"*Kommt,*" Maria urged, gesturing toward a pair of swinging doors in the wall.

Leila scampered after her. But Corey's eyes were stuck on the enormous chandeliers. He'd never seen anything like them. It seemed impossible they could stay attached to the ceiling without crashing down. The light coming through the upper windows was hitting the crystals, thousands of them. He walked into the room, watching tiny rainbows shoot out in all directions.

He was dying to show Leila, but she and Maria had disappeared behind the hinged doors. As Corey turned to follow, he heard a soft crashing noise and the click of a closing door to his right.

"Hello?"

His voice sounded small and weak in the big room. The noise came from the stage area, under the far balcony. Behind the podium and under the balcony was a door in the wall. Corey was sure someone had slipped inside.

Which meant someone was here who wasn't supposed to be.

He thought about heading into the kitchen to tell Maria, but his eyes landed on a pile of stuff—a chisel, hammer, and mound of rags at the base of a thick white pillar under the balcony.

As he stepped closer to examine, the door's handle clicked again.

Corey quickly hid behind the pillar. He heard the door squeak as it slowly swung open, and he held his breath.

He waited for footsteps, his heart galloping. He

counted to one hundred. But there were no other sounds in the room, no footsteps, no voice, no other person's breathing.

He waited a few seconds more in total silence.

Whoever had been there must have retreated. And Corey had no interest in sticking around to find out who it was. Slowly he craned his neck around the pillar.

On the other side, a thick-haired man with a beard stubble was looking back at him.

"Gahh!" Corey blurted out, jumping back.

The guy said nothing. His eyes were bloodshot, his lips thin and drawn into a horizontal line.

"L-L—Leila?" Corey rasped, backing slowly away. "*Leila?*"

With a sharp *ssshhh*, the man grabbed Corey's arm and dragged him away from the pillar and inside the open door.

10

Corey didn't know what the guy was saying. He was practically spitting his words. He seemed jittery and wild-eyed. None of those things was a good sign.

"I—I don't speak German," Corey said. "No . . . gespeaken . . ."

The guy stopped. His eyes were focused on Corey's shoes now. He swallowed and blinked. "*Bist du. . . Amerikanisch?*" he said.

"R-r—right," Corey replied. "I come in peace."

He cringed at his own words. That plea hadn't worked the first time.

"Peace," the man repeated. Then he pointed to himself. "Eh . . . Georg, me," he said, pronouncing the name *GAY-org.* "Johann Georg Elser."

"Corey, me," Corey replied.

The man gestured toward Corey's shoes. "*Sehr . . . interessant.*"

"Air Jordans," Corey said.

The guy cocked his head. "*Er . . . was?*"

Corey tried to shake loose, but the guy held tight. He wasn't sure what to do. Possibilities flew through his head: The guy could be homeless. Or a burglar. Or a repairman who got stuck in the place overnight and was afraid to be found out. Or a homicidal maniac digging graves under the restaurant.

"Well, nice to meet you," Corey said. "But I'm late for breakfast. *Leil*—!"

"*Ssssh!*" With his free hand, Georg covered Corey's mouth. The palm smelled of motor oil and plaster. Corey looked around desperately for a mode of escape. He couldn't help coughing. The only thing he could do was use his teeth. In midcough, he bit down hard. His teeth grabbed a tough, fleshy part of the guy's palm. As Georg jerked backward, gasping, Corey bolted out the door and headed for the kitchen.

"*Nein!*" Georg cried out. His hand grabbed the edge of Corey's untucked shirt. Corey lost his balance. They both tumbled to the floor, landing next to the pile of tools by the pillar. Corey reached for a hammer, but Georg snatched it away from him and held it high over his head.

Corey scrabbled to his feet. "You—you don't want to do that. I'm not even born yet."

Georg's face was growing red and swollen. His chest was heaving. "Who . . . is you?"

"A tourist?" Corey replied. Georg looked confused, but at least he had some English vocabulary, so Corey slowed down. "I . . . don't care . . . that you're . . . here. Okay? Let . . . me . . . go . . . and I won't . . . say . . . a word."

"You . . . me . . . secret?" Georg said, his voice soft and desperate sounding. "Please to tell nobody about me . . . ?"

"Absolutely nobody. Boy Scout promise." Corey began backing away. "Mouth gezippen."

"Or I must . . ."

The old guy was fishing for the right English word. But Corey didn't care what the right English word was. He turned, zigzagging around the tables toward the kitchen. He didn't bother to look back.

In the kitchen, Maria and Leila were chatting away in a mix of German and English, while Maria prepared an elaborate-looking omelet. The air smelled of cooked onions and peppers. "Where have you been?" Leila asked.

"Nowhere!" Corey snapped, a little too loud. He forced a smile, trying to stop himself from jittering. "I mean, just . . . in there. The restaurant. Ballroom. Or whatever it is. Admiring the chandeliers."

"Very biggest room, eh?" Maria said. "Are you hungry?"

"Wait, you know English?" Corey asked.

Maria laughed. "*Ja, ein bisschen.*"

"That means 'yes, a little,'" Leila said, raising an eyebrow toward Corey. "And you are lying to me. Something happened."

"Nope," Corey lied.

"What was it?" Leila insisted.

"I'm not supposed to tell you!"

Once again, Corey cringed at his own words.

With a sigh, Leila removed her apron. Taking Corey by the arm, she led him back toward the restaurant. "*Entschuldigung, Maria, er hat Angst, auf die Toilette zu gehen.*"

As they approached the door, Corey asked. "What did you tell her?"

"That you were nervous about going to the bathroom."

"That's humiliating!"

Leila pulled him through the swinging doors and into the big restaurant. Corey's eyes went right to the pillar, where he'd last seen Georg, but the guy was nowhere in sight.

"So tell me, Corey Fletcher," Leila barreled on, "why are you acting so weird? And *what just happened to you? We* are here in nineteen thirty-nine, this is *your* idea, and if you think you're going to keep secrets from me, I will go back to the future and leave you here to work things out yourself."

Corey thought for a moment. "I did a little snooping around, but . . . um . . . I promised someone I wouldn't say what I saw. Sorry. Don't leave me here."

"We're, like, a century in the past and you're worried about keeping secrets?"

"It was a guy named Georg, Leila, okay?" Corey replied. "He was doing something with tools . . . repairing . . . I don't know. It didn't seem like it would be a big deal, but he hid from me. I was curious. I didn't expect him to jump me with a hammer."

"What? He attacked you?" Leila ran around Corey, heading for the door. "No one attacks my best friend!"

"Leila, no!" Corey yelled. "Wait, I'm your best friend? *Come back!*"

There was no stopping her. Corey raced to the pillar to pick up one of the tools, just in case they needed to threaten him. But the floor around the pillar was clear—no tools, no rags, no pile of dust.

"He escaped!" Leila called out from the door. "There's no one in here."

"That was quick," Corey said. "There were tools here. A hammer, a chisel, rags. Like the guy had been repairing one of these columns."

"Repairing?" Leila said. "So he's a homicidal custodian?"

Corey knelt by the pillar. A thin rectangle had been traced into the side, about two feet high by a foot wide. Leila ran her fingers along the shape. "Looks like some kind of door. But there's no keyhole. No handle."

"You think he's hiding something in there he doesn't want Maria to know about?" Corey guessed.

"Why would a person hide something in a big old restaurant?"

Corey shrugged. "I'll work on that."

"At any rate, he probably wouldn't care about Maria. She doesn't run the place or own it. She's just a waiter, plus she cooks and shops." Leila glanced around the room. "Maybe he's still here. Maybe *he's* hiding."

"This place is huge. You could play a baseball game

in here." Corey gazed up into the balconies, looking for shadows, movement, but he saw nothing unusual. The chandelier crystals shot pinpricks of light against the wall. One of them seemed to be turning slightly, as if from a small gust of wind.

There was something about those chandeliers.

His eyes fixed on one of them. It hung from a sturdy metal ring affixed to the ceiling. From the circumference of the ring, filigreed metal bars curved downward and inward to meet at the center. They formed a cage in the shape of a half-sphere, containing a bank of light bulbs.

Removing his backpack, Corey reached inside and pulled out the rusted, twisted piece of metal, the artifact from Auntie Flora's box. He held it high, his eyes darting from it to the chandeliers. "Leila?" he said.

"What are you doing?"

"Holding up your Auntie Flora's artifact. Look at it. Then look at the chandeliers."

Adjusting for the warps and corrosion, the bent shard was a perfect match for any of the curved metal bars.

Leila gasped. "Whoa . . . it's the same."

"Which explains how this artifact got us here," Corey said.

"But why would Auntie Flora's ancestors have saved a mangled piece of a chandelier? Why did she keep it?"

"And the message that was attached to it—what did that mean?" Corey reached into his pack, pulled the photo from the decaying envelope, and flipped it to the message on the back.

CLARA, MEIN LIEBCHEN:
VERGISS NICHT.
HÖR NICHT AUF ZU VERSUCHEN
11/39
—M. STROBEL

"This stuff about never forgetting," Corey said. "Never forget what?"

"*Leila?*"

The call from the kitchen startled them both. "Breakfast break," Corey said.

"Put that thing away." Heading toward the kitchen, Leila cried out, "*Es tut mir leid, Maria!* I'm sorry!"

Corey shoved the metal back into his pack and followed Leila into the kitchen. There, Maria had set out plates piled high with fluffy, steaming omelets and piping hot cups of tea.

As Corey sat, he caught a glimpse of a calendar on

86

the wall—a portrait of a smiling milkmaid and an unsmiling cow in a field, with a date printed across the top: NOVEMBER 1939.

Corey glanced at Leila. She'd picked up on that, too. If they'd had any doubts, there was the date. The same day and month on the artifact.

"*Ess!* Eat!" Maria urged as she removed her apron and sat across from them. "This Onkel Franz? He is free tonight?"

"Onkel who?" Corey said.

Leila kicked him under the table. She gave him a look that said *just-say-yes-to-my-dumb-alibi-because-it-was-all-I-could-think-of.* "Yes, Franz. Who we are visiting in Germany. Our favorite uncle."

"The best!" Corey said, playing along. "We love him. A lot. We call him . . . Franzy Pants."

"Please, I invite to you to come. Here. Tonight," Maria said with a smile. "All three of you. I bring you dinner."

Corey shot Leila a panicked look. "Uh . . . unfortunately Uncle Franz can't come."

"Oh?" Maria said.

"He's dead," Corey blurted.

At Leila's second kick, Corey let out a gasp. "He means Franz is *sick*," Leila said. "Franz *ist krank. Danke,*

87

Maria, *aber wir müssen gehen.*" She turned to Corey. "We can't stay for dinner because we need to go to take care of him. Right, Corey?"

"I know very good doctors," Maria said.

"We need to take him away to a special hospital," Leila blurted. "Far away."

"New York," Corey improvised.

Maria nodded. "Ahhh, it is good, you leave Europe now." She gave them an uncertain look. "You of course know about Hitler?"

"Hate him," Corey shot back.

Leila kicked him a third time. Trash-talking Nazis in 1939 Germany wasn't a smart thing.

"Hate?" Maria said.

"Um, maybe hate is the wrong word?" Corey quickly replied.

But Maria's lips were curling into a smile. Lowering her voice to a conspiratorial whisper, she said, "*Das ist gut. Sehr gut.*"

"So y-you agree?" Leila whispered. "You're not a—"

"Nazi?" Maria said with a sneer. "*Nein! Aber*— You do not tell anyone I say this?"

"No way," Leila said.

"I'm all about keeping secrets," Corey added.

Maria nodded. She sat at the table and leaned toward them. "Everything in Germany bad. Very bad," She waved her fingers nervously in the air. "The country *ist ganz verrückt*. Crazy. You will not want to be near the Bürgerbräukeller when we are visited by *der Affe mit dem Schnurrbart*."

"What does that mean?" Corey asked.

"The monkey with the mustache?" Leila said, looking confused.

"It is the name I give to *der Führer*," she whispered, with a derisive snort. "That monkey Hitler. Every year he speaks here. Many people come. We will make many marks. But the Nazis—*pfft*! They take most of it anyway. Enough of this talk. *Möchtet ihr Milch?* Can I get you milk?"

Maria stood back up and pulled a small wad of bills from her pocket. "When we are *fertig*—finished— please, take this and buy some *echte deutsche Kleidung*. Proper German clothing. I insist."

She glanced quickly at Corey's and Leila's outfits, barely concealing a giggle at the sight of Corey's Air Jordans. Then she bustled to the refrigerator. She did not seem to enjoy staying still.

Corey tucked his shoes under the table. His heart,

which had been racing, was beginning to calm. He glanced at Leila, but she was staring at the apron on the counter. A tag hung from one of the straps, with a name. Quickly Leila reached toward it, pulling out the entire tag so they could see it.

The sight of the full name gave Corey a chill.

BÜRGERBRÄUKELLER
MARIA
STROBEL

11

The umbrella Corey had found in the trash was now leaking onto his head. The cheap 1939 clothes he and Leila had bought were already wet, especially the thin-soled shoes. Corey's Air Jordans were in his backpack, and he missed them.

Germans barreled down the sidewalk, bumping into him like he didn't exist. Bulky old cars farted their ways down the street, sending up geysers of black water from deep potholes. The air smelled like gasoline, and just about every one of the rushing pedestrians smoked cigarettes.

"Okay, I am totally stumped," Leila said.

Corey nodded. "You saw her name, Leila. Maria Strobel. She's the one who gave your ancestor that twisted chandelier part, with the message on the back of a tag. 'Do not forget. Do not stop trying.' Don't you think we should figure out what that means?"

"It could mean anything," Leila said. "Maybe they both waited on tables together. One of them broke a chandelier, and this was a souvenir. A little joke between them."

"If it was so little, why did it end up in Aunt Flora's belongings all these years?"

"I don't know. We are so unprepared for this. Maybe we should go back home and do a little more research. I told you we jumped into this too fast!"

"We can't leave now," Corey said. "Hitler's going to be right here in Munich, Leila. At the Burgerkinger."

"No. It's the Bürgerbräukeller." Which sounded to Corey something like Beer-gur-broi-keller, spoken by someone with a mouth full of Skittles.

Corey ducked, barely missing the jagged point of a passing broken German umbrella. "If we stay here," he said, "we won't have to search an entire country to find him. He'll walk right into our trap."

"Uh-huh. And what's our trap?"

"That's the part I don't know," Corey conceded. "But I'm thinking."

They stopped as they reached the next corner.

Looming over them, plastered onto the outer wall of a brick office building, was an enormous poster featuring a portrait of Adolf Hitler. His face was tilted upward, his eyes piercing and angry, his right hand raised rigidly toward the heavens. Behind his head was a black-and-white swastika with a red background, like a garish, hideous halo. At the bottom was a message in all caps. The only words Corey recognized were *ACHTUNG!*, which meant "attention," and BÜRGER-BRÄUKELLER. It was an ad promoting the rally.

A rowdy crowd had gathered. Most were staring up at the poster with great excitement, telling jokes, smacking each other on the back. A few of them gave Nazi salutes to the image. Someone was playing an accordion, and soon almost everyone was shouting an anthem tunelessly at the top of their lungs.

"What are they singing?" Corey asked.

"'*Deutschland über Alles,*'" Leila replied. "'Germany Above Everything.' I think that's the title. It was kind of the Nazi theme song."

"So *everyone's* a Nazi here?" Corey asked.

"Look out, Corey!" Leila said.

She reached out to him as a car honked, veering close to the curb. It sent up a spray of brownish-gray water from the gutter. Like an ocean wave, it doused

Corey and just about everyone else on the corner ahead. The song morphed into screams.

"Yechhh," Corey said, wiping the filthy water from his mouth.

"The driver did that on purpose!" Leila said.

Soaking wet and very angry, people shook their fists and screamed at the driver, who shouted something out his window. From the center of the crowd, a rock sailed through the air and broke the car's rear window with a loud smash.

"What the—?" Leila said.

"That was extreme," Corey added.

The crowd on the corner roared with approval, as the car skidded to a noisy halt. The driver, a wiry guy with a thin face and beady eyes, jumped out his door. Screaming, he ran toward the crowd, a crowbar held aloft. He held a tomato in his other hand, which he flung at the image of Hitler. It splatted square on the Führer's mustache.

There was a second man in the car, but he barely had a chance to get out the passenger door when a dozen men leaped on them both. Fists flew. In the distance police sirens echoed, but they were soon drowned out by a loud, rhythmic chorus from the crowd:

"*Sieg heil . . . sieg heil . . . sieg heil . . . sieg heil!*"

"Corey, let's get out of here before we get killed," Leila said.

She was yanking on his shirt now, and he followed her down the sidewalk away from the melee. Traffic had stopped. The narrow street was now bumper-to-bumper, resounding with the clangor of car horns. From farther down the block, a troop of soldiers in brown uniforms and jackboots came running up the street with pistols and truncheons.

Corey and Leila ran the opposite way. And they didn't stop until they got to the Bürgerbräukeller.

It was after 6:00 p.m. by the time they arrived. They were both sopping wet, their umbrellas broken and long since left behind in trash cans. People were lined up for nearly a block, waiting patiently under sturdier umbrellas. When Corey and Leila rushed toward the front door, some of them scowled and yelled at them in German. "They think we're cutting in line," Leila explained.

"We are," Corey said.

As they slipped through the door, the angry shouts faded. They were replaced by a wall of sound coming from below. More loud voices. One thing Corey had noticed: the Germans in Munich seemed to shout instead of talk. As he and Leila descended the stairs into the restaurant, at least three tables were full of people singing at the top of their lungs. A brass band with an accordion and a loud tuba played oompah-pah music as they wandered among the guests.

Maria was taking orders on a notepad, from a table full of boisterous gray-haired men who were clinking their beer steins and shouting to each other in German. Seeing Corey and Leila, she immediately left the table to greet them. "Hallo, *komm herein!* Come in, come in! You must eat! You are so wet! And, Corey, what happened to your *neue Kleidung?*"

"That's 'new clothing,'" Leila explained to Corey, then turned back to Maria. "He got splashed. Look, we'll talk later, Maria. You're working."

Maria looked back toward her table with a sly smile. "Pah. These men, they do not notice. They never remember what they order. If I bring them plates of boiled rat, they eat it and say *Danke schön*, Maria. So. Tell me, children, are you okay? *Ist etwas los?*"

"We saw a riot on a street corner," Corey said. "This crowd attacked some guy who was protesting Hitler's rally at the Burgerbeeger . . . beerkegger . . . *here.*"

"Hitler . . ." Maria's brash, trumpetlike voice became practically a whisper. "Yes, yes. Every year it is worse."

"Maria! *Schnell!*" shouted a heavyset man standing next to a nearby table. He was about four inches shorter than Corey, wearing a suit that was a size too small and a swastika band around his upper arm. The thickness of his waxed mustache clashed with the thinness of his hair, which was combed over his scalp like black harp strings. He smiled like a man who hated smiling.

"*Moment mal, Dummkopf!*" Maria shot back. With a wry grin, she turned to Corey and Leila. "That means 'Wait, you dumb-head.' He is my boss, Herr Schmuckler." She pulled Corey and Leila away from the table, into a more isolated area near the kitchen. Leaning in, she dropped her voice to a whisper. "Hear, please. I tell you one time. Let us not talk about Hitler and this crazy Nazi Party when *es gibt* many people like this. That was my mistake. People are listening. Now please use my rooms upstairs to clean up. Door two oh eight. You can wait and I bring you food. But it will be long night. Are you hungry?"

"Not really," Leila said.

"*Yes!*" Corey blurted over her.

"Then you must not wait," Maria said. "When you are ready, go to the bar. I will serve you dinner. *Kostenlos.*"

As she scurried away, Corey asked, "What does '*Kostenlos*' mean?"

"Free," Leila replied.

"Twist. My. Arm."

Corey was already heading for the stairs.

A meal of boiled sauerbraten, mushy asparagus, and canned orange juice in a crowded Munich bar felt like dining on the Times Square subway tracks in August. Men were dancing on tables, some wearing napkins tied into bonnets. The accordion player was pouring beer into the bell of the tuba. The floor was sticky wherever you walked, and everything smelled of cigarette smoke. The menu listed pig intestines, and Leila barely missed being hit in the head by a flying, half-eaten goose shank. If there were a Hades for time travelers, the Bürgerbräukeller at night was it.

"Beeeooo . . . boooeeeeger-broi-keller . . ." Corey said, trying for the hundredth time to pronounce the place's name. The äu sound was easy—you just said oy. But the ü sound was impossible.

Behind the bar, a bartender named Wolfgang burst out laughing at Corey's attempt. "Ist funny boy!"

"Just purse your lips like you're going to say 'oo' . . . and then say 'ee' through that," Leila said.

"Oozoo for yee to say," Corey grumbled.

He pushed his plate aside and took one last sip of

juice, which was beginning to taste like tinfoil and ash. Corey was dying for the crowd to dwindle. Then he and Leila could get more information from Maria about the rally.

He glanced around the room, at the sea of swastikas on armbands. They seemed to flitter at the tables like cockroaches. He wondered if Maria was the only one here, among thousands, who hated the Führer. So far the only anti-Nazis he'd seen were her and the guys in the car at the street corner. If there were more, they'd probably be in hiding. Was there some kind of under-ground resistance group in Munich? If she were part of that, she'd have great information. They could all brainstorm. There had to be a way to get to Hitler, right here in 1939.

"Sometimes I hate the past," Corey said. "I want to just reach into my pocket, get my phone, and find out exactly what happened here."

"Coming here wasn't what we expected to do," Leila reminded him. "How are you feeling? No bad symptoms yet, right? Why don't we just go back to the present, collect historical research, and then return here? Just like you suggested—"

"*Ssshh.*" Corey was staring at Maria, who was argu-ing with a drunken-looking man in a tattered raincoat.

By now, many of the customers had left or were heading to the door, so her voice was sharp and loud. She tried to hold the man back but he staggered toward the bar, colliding with a table full of plates of half-finished desserts. The oompah band had played their last song and were packing up. Summoned by the commotion, Herr Schmuckler rushed to Maria's side. He began pulling the drunken man back toward the door. "What are they saying?" Corey asked.

"They're telling the guy it's nine forty-five, the kitchen closed fifteen minutes ago, and they're not seating anyone," Leila replied.

As Herr Schmuckler accompanied the guy out of the restaurant, Maria stopped at the front door. She greeted a new customer who stood alone, smoking a cigar and wearing a wet trench coat and a wide-brimmed hat that hid his face.

The moment Herr Schmuckler went outside with the drunk, Maria gestured for the new customer to follow her. She led him to a small table by the kitchen. As he sat he removed his hat, revealing a fox-like face with thick hair and dark features. "Wait. Is she seating that guy?" Leila said. "I thought the kitchen was—"

"That's him!" Corey blurted.

"Who?" Leila shot back.

"The creepy guy I saw in the other room."

"Wait, the custodian killer? He's a customer?"

Corey grabbed a cloth napkin and tied it around his head like a kerchief. "I don't want him to recognize me."

"You look ridiculous," Leila said.

Ignoring her, Corey narrowed his eyes and glanced over in that direction. People were walking to and fro, sometimes blocking his view. But he could see Maria leaning close to the guy, nodding very seriously and writing things down on her pad. "Leila, do you notice anything weird?" Corey whispered.

"Besides the fact that the kitchen is closed, they're kicking people out, and she's still letting him order?"

"No, about Maria. She's always so loud and friendly with the customers. She jokes with them, insults them, makes them laugh."

"That's kind of her brand," Leila said.

"Right. But she's so quiet and serious with this guy," Corey said.

As Maria returned to the bar, she shook her head with a look of exasperation. "You know that guy?" Leila asked.

"Of course I know Herr Elser," she muttered. "He is staying with my friends, Alfons and Rosa, so I am friendly to him, but, *ach*, why does he always eat so late? I will see if the chef is in a good mood . . . meanwhile, *bitte*, Wolfgang! *Geben Sie diesen Kindern Strudel!* He will give you strudel before they put it away. It is my favorite."

As Maria disappeared into the kitchen, Wolfgang obediently reached into a small refrigerator behind the bar. He served Corey and Leila both enormous plates of apple strudel each with a scoop of vanilla ice cream.

That, at least, tasted good.

Corey kept sneaking glances toward the mysterious guy, who was peacefully reading a newspaper while the restaurant emptied. People stepped up to the bar and said *guten Nacht* to Wolfgang, leaving him tips. Winking at Corey and Leila, the bartender slipped them another serving.

Scarfing down more dessert, Corey yawned. It was getting harder and harder to stay awake.

"Corey . . . ?" Leila said. "Where's Maria?"

"Huh?" Corey said, shaking some energy into himself.

"She hasn't brought that guy his meal yet," she

replied, gesturing toward the opposite end of the restaurant, "and he's gone."

Corey was wide awake now. He whirled on his stool.

Herr Elser's table was empty, as if no one had been there all night.

12

The rain had let up. The air outside felt like an Arctic blast after the sweaty, overheated restaurant. Corey shivered as he and Leila crept around the brick building. Their eyes scanned the walls for extra doors, or any method that Georg Elser could have used to enter or escape.

At the rear of the building, Leila found a wooden hatch with open diagonal doors. Inside, steps led down into the kitchen. "Aha!" she exclaimed.

"Aha what?" Corey said. "We were sitting near the kitchen and we didn't see him go in. Maybe he snuck out the front when we weren't looking?"

"I had my eye on the front of the restaurant," Leila

said. "I would have seen him. I swear, he never left this place."

"We could look at the surveillance cameras."

"Ha ha. I have some ideas. Come on."

Leila sped back into the Bürgerbräukeller through the front door. She led Corey down the inner stairs and back into the restaurant. A couple of workers were still mopping floors and stacking chairs, and Wolfgang was counting cash at the bar.

Waving a quick hello, Leila made her way to the stage area and went right to the door behind the podium. "This is where the guy hid from you, right?" she said, yanking the door open.

"Not so fast—!"

Corey flinched, half expecting the guy to jump out with a hammer. But Leila stepped inside and flicked on the light to reveal a totally empty room. The piano and chair were exactly as Corey remembered them.

"Okay, so he's not here," Leila said. "That eliminates one possibility. Are there any other rooms?"

She turned. Directly across the stage area was another door, a mirror image of the one they'd just opened. Leila ran to that one and pulled it open. They both stared into a long, cement-walled hallway that led deeper into the building, in the direction of the kitchen.

Carefully, quietly, they stepped in, their footsteps rapping sharply against the hard floor. Before long they came to another door. Beyond it were the sounds of clinking glasses and rushing water. Corey pushed it open into a steaming back room of the kitchen, where a team of workers were hand-washing plates and glasses.

To their right, another flight of stairs led up into the higher floors of the Bürgerbräukeller. It was the same stairs Corey and Leila had taken to get to room 208, Maria's room.

"Do you think he went up there . . . ?" Leila said. "It's all, like, apartments. And he doesn't live here. Maria said he was staying with people she knew. And when he came in to dinner, he was wet from the rain."

"He's not washing plates down here," Corey said with a shrug. "So he must be up there. I think he's hiding, sneaking around. He was here this morning when Maria unlocked the place. The restaurant should have been empty."

"Wait, you think he comes here for dinner, hides out in the building until the restaurant closes, and then sneaks out in the morning when the place opens?"

Corey nodded. "He's up to something. And if he is

hiding out, I'm worried about Maria. He seemed kind of like a maniac."

"I'm not liking this one bit," Leila said.

"If anything bad happens, I can always microhop and fix it," Corey said.

"Now you want to time travel?" Leila looked at him in disbelief. "Curb your enthusiasm, Superman. We have to reserve your powers, remember?"

Together they climbed the stairs to the second floor and emerged into a long hallway lined with dark wood. It smelled musty and slightly moldy, with an open window at the other end providing the only ventilation.

At room 208, Corey rapped on the door. "Maria?"

He heard a murmur of voices within. A moment later Maria appeared at the door with a smile. She had changed from her waiter uniform into a plain button-down shirt and a pair of khaki pants. Her room was dark except for a lamp on a desk, over which a sheer scarf had been draped, bathing the room in red. "*Willkommen!* Come in!" She gestured into the room. "You come to say good-bye? Franz is here?"

"Franz?" Corey asked.

"Your *Onkel*," Maria said.

Leila exhaled. She gave Corey a long look and

stepped into the room. "Maria, we have something to tell you. I mean, after you finish closing up the restaurant."

"My work is done. The others do late work because I do shopping in the morning." Maria sat, looking at them expectantly. Four tapered candles cast soft light across her face. On her table was a brownish rectangular board. It was covered with letters and mystical symbols. On top of that was a kidney-shaped object about the size of Corey's hand, supported by four tiny legs. "Please. Sit. I was just about to contact my Horst."

"You have a horse?" Corey asked.

Maria looked at him oddly. "Horst was *mein* husband. He died sixteen years ago. We talk, through my Ouija board. You know these boards? Very popular in America. Place fingers on the planchette and the dead spell out answers to your questions. The dead, they are still with us, *meine Kinder*. The past is *Jetzt*—now. But you sit. They will wait for me. Horst is patient." She smiled. "You do not think I am crazy?"

"No. I don't." As Corey sat slowly on the bed, he thought about his trip into 1862 Central Park, 2001 downtown New York City, and 1917 Greenwich Village. "Sometimes I speak to the dead too. People in the past."

Leila shot him a wary look. But Maria just nodded

and smiled. She took his hand and Leila's. "*Ja,* I know this about you."

"You do?" Leila said.

"I know too that you do not have this Onkel Franz. *Ja?*"

Corey cleared his throat nervously. "*Ja.*"

"You are not so good at telling lies!" Maria said with a laugh. "Maria tells you *der Wahrheit.* The truth. Maria tells everybody the truth. Except, sometimes, foolish drunken German men at the Bürgerbräukeller. So you are to tell me truth, *ja?*"

"We . . . can't," Leila replied.

Maria cocked her head. "*Warum?*"

"Why? Because you wouldn't believe it," Leila said.

"How do you know?" Maria smiled. "Try me. I do not bite."

Leila look uncertainly at Corey.

"Would you think we were crazy," Corey said cautiously, "if we told you we're from the future?"

"Corey!" Leila said.

"*Was bedeutet* 'future'?" Maria asked.

"She's asking what that means," Leila said. "Zukunft, Maria."

"We are from the Zukunft . . . twenty-first century," Corey continued.

Maria's smile fell. She looked deeply into Corey's eyes, then Leila's. "*Das ist ja die Wahrheit?*"

Leila took a deep breath. "*Ja*. It's the truth."

Maria stood and turned away from them, her hand on her chin.

"She thinks we're loony birds," Corey whispered. "I knew it. We should have stuck with Uncle Franzy Pants."

"*Mein Vaterland* . . . my fatherland, Germany . . ." Maria blurted out. "So much bad things now. Kristall-nacht . . . you know this? Last year they take away the Jews, smash their windows, steal everything." Maria looked pleadingly at Leila, then Corey. "The Zukunft . . . future. Tell me about this. Does these Nazis . . . ?" Her voice drifted off.

"Succeed?" Leila said. "Take over the world? No. But they come close. The entire world becomes involved in a war. Thousands of soldiers die. Millions of Jews, not to mention Poles, gay people, anyone they hate . . . all slaughtered in cold blood. In death camps."

"*Ach, mein Gott*," Maria said, her voice dropping to a whisper. "This cannot happen."

"You wanted to know why we were here," Corey said. He took a deep breath and sat up ramrod straight. "The truth is, I have a power. A superpower, really.

I can change the past. We came here to stop Hitler. We travel through time using metal artifacts. Like this one."

He reached into his pack and pulled out the corroded old metal shank. Maria took it, not knowing what to make of it. "What is this thing?"

"We think it's part of a chandelier in the restaurant," Corey said. "We also found a note from you to someone named Clara. Who is Clara?"

"*Meine Freundin*," Maria replied. "My friend."

"Help us, Maria," Corey said. "I can change history, if I have a plan. But I don't know what to do."

"I—I—" Maria's voice caught in her throat. Her eyes were drawn upward, to something behind Leila's and Corey's shoulders.

That was when Corey heard the thump of a footstep.

He whirled around to see in the doorway a scowling woman with high cheekbones and hair pulled back into a ponytail.

"Clara?" Maria said with a quizzical look. "*Alles in Ordnung? Was ist los?*"

From behind her stepped Georg Elser, aiming a pistol at Corey's head.

13

"Do not . . . do anything . . . dumb," Leila murmured to Corey.

The only thing Corey was doing was putting his hands in the air. He couldn't think of anything else under the circumstances.

Maria, Clara, and Georg were all crowded into the room now, the door shut behind them. They were chattering away in German, their voices hushed and urgent. Corey could swear he recognized the word Zukunft. Georg was waving the gun wildly.

"If he's not careful, he'll shoot the person next door through the wall," Corey whispered.

"If he's not careful, he'll shoot us," Leila replied.

"What are they saying?"

"The guy is calling us *Hitlerjugend*. He thinks we're Hitler Youth."

"*What?*" Corey turned toward the group, waving his hands. "*Nein! Nein! Nein!*"

Georg glared at him, aiming the pistol at Corey again.

"That's not helping," Leila said.

"*Elser, du Schwein, steck das weg!*" Maria added. "Put it away!"

Georg's eyes shifted uneasily between the two women. He scowled at Corey, flipped the safety on, and dropped the gun in a black leather shoulder sack.

Clara stuck out her hand toward Corey and Leila. "So sorry, bit of a misunderstanding," she said in a clipped accent that seemed both German and British. "Herr Elser was under the impression that you two were working for the Nazis."

"So . . . he and you are like Maria?" Corey said, shaking the woman's hand. "Anti-Nazi?"

"*Ja.* You'd be surprised how many children have been recruited to turn on their neighbors and families," the woman replied. "Please. Forgive our rudeness. I am Clara Scharfstein."

Hearing the last name, Corey's jaw dropped. Leila's words were still fresh in his mind. *Did you know Opa's name was Josef Scharfstein, and he changed it to Sharp at Ellis Island?*

"No. Way," he murmured.

Leila's face had gone ashen. Corey thought she would faint. "Of course!" she blurted. "That's why Auntie Flora had the artifact. It came from you! You're my great-great-aunt Or maybe great! Of course! I should have known. You—you look like Auntie Flora! I can tell, it's in the nose!"

She leaped at Clara. The woman flinched, but she didn't have room to move away before Leila wrapped her in an impulsive hug, squealing with amazement and joy. Maria's somber face broke into a smile, but Georg seemed confused and Clara looked trapped.

"She's fan-girling," Corey explained.

"Yes. Well." Clara pulled loose from Leila and patted her hand. "Maria tells me you are to be trusted. And so Georg and I will trust you, too. I am the leader of *Der Münchenfrauenwiderstand*."

"Can you say that slowly?" Corey asked.

"You may call us the MFW," Clara replied. "It means Munich Women's Resistance. We will explain why Georg is here. But it is necessary that our secrecy is absolute. You must promise me that with your lives."

"Definitely," Leila said.

"Yup," Corey agreed.

"Because, you know, just now Maria has confided a secret about you, too," Clara said. "Some rather fanciful things about your visit. An elaborate science experiment, yes? Visitors from *die Zukunft*? Tell me more."

Leila and Corey both glanced toward Maria, but her eyes never wavered from Clara. Corey swallowed, not knowing what to expect. "Uh, well . . . we're from New York City, in the twenty-first century."

Clara nodded. "Did you perhaps . . . emerge from Maria's Ouija board?"

"Clara, *bitte!*" Maria snapped.

"We are being honest, yes?" Clara said. "Maria is dedicated to her *Spiritismus*, I am more a scientist. I have heard Herr Einstein speak on the puzzles of time and space. But time travel?" She smiled tightly. "This is difficult to accept without proof."

Corey reached into his pocket and took out his Air Jordans. "Would anyone wear something like this in nineteen thirty-nine?"

Clara grimaced at the sight of the sneakers. Or maybe the smell. But Leila grabbed the metal rod and the photo from where Maria had left them on the bed.

"This stuff was inherited by my aunt," Leila said, "who is descended from Clara."

"I know this design . . ." Georg said, holding the artifact up to the lamp light.

Clara took the note, but unlike Maria she turned it over to see the photo. She stared intently at the two figures posing. "These women . . ." she said, shaking her head. "They are you and me, Mariaschen. But . . . *so alt*. Old. And our hair . . . why does it look like that?"

"Those are *you*?" Corey slipped behind her and looked over her shoulder. Earlier he hadn't made any kind of mental connection with that photo. The two women were heavier and much older than Maria and Clara. But now, having met them, he saw that the resemblance was unmistakable.

Maria came to their side. At the sight of the image, her eyes widened. "*Ach du Lieber*. That gate. I have seen photos of one like it."

Clara nodded. "Auschwitz."

"The camps became historical sites," Leila said softly. "After the war ended. The hairstyle is from, like, the late nineteen sixties or early nineteen seventies, I think."

Clara's hand was shaking as she turned the photo over and read the inscription. "That is Maria's handwriting. How baffling and strange. Tell me, when does the war end?"

"Nineteen forty-five," Leila replied.

Georg's face went pale. "Hitler lives?"

"He dies," Leila replied. "But not for another five or six years."

Corey nodded. "And millions of people are killed. In places like Auschwitz. I want to change that. I have the power to do it. Can you tell us about this piece of metal? We think it comes from one of the chandeliers."

"*Ja, sicher*," Georg said, placing the shard back on the bed. "It is from the Bürgerbräukeller."

"When we first got here," Leila said, "Corey found Georg sneaking around in the restaurant. So we're trying to put all of this together."

Maria took a deep breath and glanced at Clara. She nodded, as if giving Maria permission.

"All right, I tell you about Georg," Maria said. "One morning I am opening the restaurant early. Much more early than I always do. I do not expect to see anyone. But there is Georg. He is putting hole in . . . *wie sagt man Säule?*"

"Column," Clara said. "Or pillar."

Corey nodded. "Right. Hole in column. We saw that."

"Georg was angry! He almost kill me for finding him!" Maria said. "But I talk to him. I know his face. In a few minutes I know why. He and my husband, Horst, they work together many years ago, in woodworking shop in Königsbronn. As I told you, in nineteen twenty-three Horst died, fighting the Nazis— right here in Munich, at the Bürgerbräukeller. They call this fight the Beer Hall Putsch. But the Nazis lose this fight, and Hitler goes to jail. I do not stop crying for a week because of Horst. I hate them for what they did. Still, in those days most people think the Nazis are small group. Crazy monsters. They will go away! But . . ." Maria threw her hands in the air. "They get power anyway, many years later. So Georg knows I do not like Hitler. He does not like Hitler. And we become . . . *Freunde*."

"Friends," Leila said.

"Accomplices," Corey added.

"In the Nazis' twisted minds," Clara said, "this Beer Hall Putsch defeat becomes some kind of great moment. The dead soldiers are martyrs. And now, every year in honor of this battle, Hitler comes here to make a speech. To gloat."

"And Georg . . . ?" Corey asked.

Clara barked a few words of German to Georg. For a moment he glowered at Corey, then gave an uncertain

118

glance back to Clara. Finally, with a sigh, he opened his sack and took out a sheaf of white graph paper.

Carefully he laid them out next to one another on the floor.

One of them showed a blueprint of the Bürgerbräukeller building, with all the balconies, doors, tunnels, and inner rooms marked out. Another showed the architecture of the grand hall—the table layouts, the pillars, the chandeliers. A big red circle was drawn on the pillar next to the stage.

Corey and Leila leaned into the last two sheets. One displayed a cross section of the pillar. It was hollow on the inside, with a rectangular area measured and removed. The other sheet showed a complicated electrical circuit connected to some kind of machine. "So wait," Corey said. "You're, like, hollowing out the pillar. And putting in this electrical thingie?"

Georg cocked his head. "Singie?"

"Georg Elser is a man of many talents," Clara said softly, "and he has been working for months. Sometimes, as you see, over a drafting table. Sometimes in the forest, where no one can hear things that ought not to be heard. Sometimes in a woodworking shop not far from here. There he is creating a container for his miraculous invention. He shall put it all to use right here in the Bürgerbräukeller, in the greatest triumph of his life."

"Which is what?" Corey said.

"Some kind of bug? Wiretap? Listening device?" Leila asked.

Georg shot Clara and Maria an uncertain look, but they both held his glance. "Go on, answer them, Herr Elser," Clara said. "It is the same word in English as it is in German."

Georg spoke so quietly they could barely hear him. But the word could not have been more clear.

"*Bombe.*"

Corey gulped. "I'm thinking that means bomb."

"That's what this is all about?" Leila asked. "A plot to kill Hitler?"

"A plot that doesn't work, apparently," Clara said.

Georg looked on the verge of tears. "*Es wird ein Versager sein.*"

"He's saying it will be a failure," Leila translated.

"No," Corey said, smiling confidently. "This is a job for a Throwback."

14

Brög sounded like the name of a video game character. And he looked it, too.

At the break of dawn, as Corey and Leila entered the woodworking shop at the edge of town, a flannel-shirted man with an ax over his shoulder grunted a greeting. He stood about seven feet tall with shoulders nearly as wide, his frame silhouetted in orange by the flames of an oven behind him. He stared at them through ice-blue eyes from under a mass of unruly black hair, his eyebrows thick like raven's wings.

"*Morgen*, Brög," said Georg.

"*Willkommen! Willkommen!*" the man bellowed, his beard jittering like a giant agitated possum. "*Die Schöne und das Biest.* HAAWWW! HAW! HAW! HAW!"

"He is calling us beauties and the beast," Georg said. "Like children's story. It is joke. Brög enjoys the joking."

"We got that," Corey said dryly.

Brög brought his ax down hard. It instantly shattered a wood stump, the pieces of which he tossed into the oven like they were scraps of paper.

"Maybe," Leila murmured, "we should politely laugh."

"*Kommt, kommt*," Brög said.

Georg went into the shop first. The walls were lined with shelves, and several counters and tables were crammed with hammers, pliers, wrenches, vises, and some frightening-looking tools that looked like dental implements for a giant.

"Cool," Corey said.

Leila exhaled. "We shouldn't be here."

"We need to be involved, Leila. We have a chance to help him."

"Help him *kill someone*, Corey," Leila said.

"You're having second thoughts?" Corey asked.

"Shouldn't I?" Leila shot back. "What part of 'Thou shalt not kill' don't you get?"

"I totally get it," Corey said. "I can't stop thinking about it. My stomach is in a knot. I threw up in the bathroom twice, before we came here."

"The bathroom we're *sharing?*" Leila shouted.

"I cleaned up, your highness," Corey said. "But that's how crazy nervous I am, okay? I know about good and evil. But we can't forget. Hitler was one of the worst mass murderers in history. By not helping Georg, we're allowing people to die. And that's more wrong. Right?"

"Well, yeah. But why can't he do it himself?" Leila asked. "Without us?"

"Because this bombing *did not work,*" Corey said. "If it did, Hitler would have died. We also know it destroyed that chandelier. Which means the explosion went off. What happened? Did the timer fail? Did he escape?"

"*Kinder! Kommt!*" Brög called from deep inside the shop, gesturing for Corey and Leila to join him and Georg. They were standing at a set of shelves, where Georg was examining a wooden box.

Georg smiled as he ran his hands over the box's surface. "It is simple. Beautiful. I work on this for many weeks. Brög helps me. Inside goes the *Bombe.* But it makes tick-tick-tick . . . people hear."

"The timer," Corey said. "You're saying that you're worried about the ticking of the timer."

"*Ja,*" Georg replied. "Now look." On one side of the

box was a small door with a tiny handle, and Georg pulled it open. Inside, it was packed with a thick, black, rubbery substance.

"Ha HA!" Brög blurted out. "*Ganz still!*"

"'Completely quiet,'" Leila translated.

"Insulation," Corey said.

"Yes. This is last thing I need for plan." Georg shut the door of the contraption and slipped Brög a thick wad of bills. "*Danke, mein Freund.*"

"Leila, did you see that?" Corey remarked under his breath. "That looks like a fortune."

"Maybe not," Leila said. "German money wasn't worth too much before the war."

The two men huddled near the fireplace, talking in muted German. Brög cast quick glances toward Corey and Leila.

"What's he saying?" Corey asked.

"I can't tell," Leila replied. "Something about a train trip."

Now Georg was heading for them, walking quickly. "We go now. Brög cannot stay here. I cannot stay here. After *die Bombe*, Nazis will look for us. I give Brög enough for train trip to Stuttgart and hotel."

As they headed outside, the sidewalk was empty. The streetlamps cast small pools of amber light. "So now you have the last thing you needed," Corey said. "What's your plan?"

Georg put his finger to his mouth, eyeing the buildings around them. His pace was brisk. He didn't say a word as they trudged back through the empty streets. Approaching the Bürgerbräukeller, Corey could see that his entire body was shaking. "Hey, it's going to be okay," he said.

Georg spun around, as if he'd forgotten Corey was there. The bag with the contraption slipped from his hands. He let out a gasp and flailed to grab it back.

Leila lurched forward, snatching the bag before it hit the pavement. "Whoa. Easy, Mr. Elser," she said. "You don't want to blow us up."

Georg rested his arm against the side of the Bürgerbräukeller archway. He took deep breaths. "*Entschuldigung.* I am sorry. It is a long time I am planning. Much dangerous. I hold much secrets."

"You can tell us any secrets," Leila whispered. "I mean, you don't have to. But we're here to help you, remember?"

The man eyed the surroundings nervously. Then he swallowed and spoke in a whisper. "I work for months. I find material. I test *die Bombe* in the woods, where nobody hears. I fix pillar. I work in Bürgerbräukeller until morning. Day for day, week for week. Every day I worry someone sees me, someone tells Nazis. They will shoot me. It makes me feel . . . I don't know how to say . . ."

"Nervous," Leila said. "*Nervös.*"

"*Ja, nervös,*" Georg repeated.

"It'll all be over soon," Corey said.

In the damp air, Georg's head seemed shrouded in mist. "I was not afraid before today. Now you bring me part of chandelier. You tell me Hitler does not die."

"Yeah, but it doesn't have to be that way," Corey said. "That's why I'm here. You have to trust me. I can change history. I've done it before. If Hitler dies, you will be a hero for all time."

Georg let out a deep sigh. Under the streetlamp, in the damp air, his head seemed shrouded in mist. He looked confused, torn between hope and skepticism. "I do not see how you will know what to change. You tell me you do not know what went wrong."

Leila looked at Corey. He tried to give her and Georg a brave, confident smile.

But Corey didn't feel brave at that moment. And he didn't feel confident. The words stung. Georg was right. This was not like trying to thwart a robbery. It wasn't like saving a pet from being run over. The stakes here were crazy.

And maybe he and Leila were crazy, too. Trying to kill a monster was one thing. Doing it in a crowded restaurant full of Nazis—without a plan—was another.

There were limits to superpowers.

"So . . ." Leila said. "Tell us everything, Georg. All the details about Wednesday night. *Mittwoch Abend*."

"Hitler's speech begins at eight thirty," Georg said. "He will talk two hours. But Hitler . . . he sometimes talks all night."

"So he'll finish ten thirty at the earliest?" Leila said.

"*Ja*," Georg replied. "There will be many people. They all want to say hello, *Heil Hitler*. . . . I do not think he starts on time. Maybe eight forty-five, maybe nine."

"How many people?" Corey asked.

"*Vielleicht drei tausend*," Georg said.

"Three thousand people in a closed room with a bomb?" Leila said. "This sounds insane."

"*Nein*," Georg said. "I test *die Bombe*. Many times. In four meters around, is dangerous. That is where Hitler will be. And the other Nazis. The customers? Closest will be ten meters."

"How can you be sure?" Leila said.

"Maria will have tables more than ten meters away," Georg said. "With rope. She tells Nazi soldiers to protect the Führer. They will be like . . . *Schilde?*"

"'Shields,'" Leila said.

"*Bombe* must not go off early. So we set timer for nine twenty." Georg turned and looked through the archway toward the restaurant. "Maria will let us in now. Then she must lock up. You go to your rooms. I hide. It is early. The night guard has left. I will install *die Bombe.*"

"We," Corey said.

"We?" Leila said.

"We're a team," Corey replied.

Georg stood and turned toward the Bürgerbräukeller. A tear ran down his cheek. "I am sorry. Germans do not cry. But I have many *Gefühle.* Emotions. *In zwei Tagen stirbt der Affe.*"

Corey cocked his head. "And that means . . . ?"

"In two days," Leila translated, "the monkey dies."

As Georg turned to walk through the gate, Leila followed. She gave Corey a glance over her shoulder.

He tried to give her a confident smile. But he realized he was clenching and unclenching his hands. He looked down and stretched them out. They were the way they'd always been. None of the signs of transspeciation he'd been warned about.

As he followed the other two into the building, a thought began forming in his head. Failure wasn't really an option here. Knowledge was power. And knowledge about what happened Wednesday night was a quick time hop away.

Maybe Leila's suggestion was right.

A Throwback had to do what a Throwback had to do.

15

Corey tried not to make noise, but it felt like his lungs were having a boxing match in his chest. He lay still on a carpeted floor, grimacing. For a moment he didn't know where he was. If he moved even a muscle, he knew he'd groan. And if he groaned, someone would hear him.

So he lay still.

The shock to the system seemed to get worse with each time hop, not better. When did this get easier? Shouldn't it get easier?

After a few minutes, he slowly sat up in the living room of his Upper West Side home. Light filtered in from the street, and he could see an outline of the old clock, just now striking 1:00 a.m.

Just as he expected, it didn't make a sound.

Being home, taking a break from Nazi Germany, should have felt great. But Corey wanted to get in and get out, fast and quiet. He just needed information, that's all. It wouldn't take much to find out what happened on November 8, 1939, at that beer hall in Munich, Germany.

He removed the phone from his pocket and powered it on. Immediately it lit up with notifications, a chorus of *ping! ping! ping!* that might wake up his whole family. He quickly shut off the sound. His charger was still where he'd left it, so he plugged in his phone and navigated straight to the photos he's taken before he'd time-traveled back to the present.

They were still there, every one. Every photo he had sneaked after following Leila and Georg back into the Bürgerbräukeller. The entire sprawling, empty restaurant. A close-up of the inside of the hollowed-out pillar. The wiring. The clock timer. The almost invisible rectangular seam when the whole thing was sealed up.

Wi-Fi and cell service may have been decades away in 1939 Germany, but since Corey's phone still powered on, he could take photos and save them to the phone's drive.

Right now, they served as a record of a perfect crime that failed. Something in the wiring, the placement, the technology—*something* had to give a hint what went wrong.

His fingers navigated to search.

> 🔍 **GEORG ELSER BOMBING**

Corey scrolled through all the entries, reading as many as he could, soaking up the history. Elser was the oldest of six, great at drawing and math, but his father drank and his parents divorced. As a young adult he worked in furniture, woodworking, clocks, carpentry, armaments. He made housings for wall and table clocks. He got a job in a shipping company where he had access to fuses and detonators.

It all made total sense. Elser's personal life seemed like a mixed bag, but his professional life was like . . . clockwork.

Corey skipped lightly over all that stuff. Sure enough, every online biography of Elser included information about November 8, 1939. Plenty of it, in great detail. What went right and what went wrong. Corey pored over every word.

The bomb had worked. The problem had to do with timing.

On that day, Hitler was deep into his plans for war with France. He wanted to cancel the speech at the Bürgerbräukeller completely. It came very close to not happening at all. But the tradition was long and Hitler loved a big, adoring crowd. So at the last minute he changed his mind. After he decided yes, he *would* do it, his staff told him the weather wouldn't be suitable for flying back to Berlin the next day. So if he really wanted to give the speech, he would have to take the train that night. And the train would have to leave at 9:30 p.m.

Which meant Hitler would not start at 8:30 as planned. He'd start a half hour early, at 8:00 p.m. sharp. And he'd speak for only an hour.

That night, unlike his usual rambling self, he pretty much stuck to schedule. He started around 8:00 and ended at 9:07.

Which was thirteen minutes before Georg Elser had set the timer to detonate the bomb, at 9:20.

Corey felt the blood draining from his head. *That* was how Hitler escaped.

He'd have to show this research to Leila, Georg, Maria, and Clara. He saved the articles to his Files folder, hoping they would be there when he went to 1939. The photos would help, too, so he included what he could find. Like images of the bomb mechanism and the restaurant before and after the explosion. A photo of the destruction gave him goose bumps. This was real. And dangerous.

He was concentrating so hard he didn't notice someone entering the room.

"Want some olives?"

At the sound of Zenobia's voice, Corey nearly dropped his phone. She was standing in the doorway to the kitchen, picking with her fingers from with a plastic container of brown olives from the Mani Market.

"You scared me," he said. "What are you doing awake at 1 a.m. eating olives?"

Zenobia shrugged. "I had a craving. Why are you wearing those clothes?" With a sly grin, she sat on the arm of the couch. "Are you guys doing *Newsies*? Or is this the way you dress when you use a dating app for toddlers?"

Corey quickly swiped up to make the photos disappear. "I thought you said you weren't going to make fun of me anymore. After I saved you."

"Just joking. Jeez, you are so serious." She cocked her head curiously. "Hey, are you okay? You don't look so good."

"That's because I'm looking at you eating olives with your fingers."

"Ha ha. There are plenty more." She held out the open container. "They taste even better marinated in finger sweat."

"Sounds delicious, but I have to go."

Zenobia let out a laugh. "Go where? It's one in the morning."

From farther inside the apartment, Corey heard a groan and a thump. Zenobia glanced back over her shoulder. "Mom?"

Corey heard a yawn, and it wasn't his mom's. A familiar voice called out, "Will you please stop making so much noi—"

Zenobia leaped up from the sofa, sending olives all over the living room.

Corey held tight to his phone. But the blood was rushing from his head.

Standing the doorway, staring at him like some twisted 3D-mirroring app, was Corey Fletcher.

"This wasn't supposed to happen," Corey murmured.

"I know," said the other Corey.

"How did I mess this one up? Every time I time hop back to where I started, I just exchange places with myself. There's always one Corey. This never happened before."

The other Corey shrugged. "Time travel can be sloppy, I guess. Maybe your powers are evolving." He laughed. "My powers."

"Our powers."

Corey had been curious about what it would be like to talk to himself. It felt terrible. It felt like some small creature had crawled inside him and was twanging all his nerves, head to toe, like a guitar.

They both glanced toward Zenobia, who was now

on the floor, unconscious. "I didn't know people actually fainted in real life," the other Corey remarked.

"Would you take care of her?" Corey asked. "I—I have to go."

The other Corey nodded. He picked up the backpack from the floor and handed it over. "I know."

Corey quickly unplugged his phone and pocketed it. Then he reached inside for the chandelier shard, which was practically too hot to touch. But he forced his hand around it, allowing the heat to soothe his nerves while it singed his skin.

The last thing he saw before blacking out was his own back, dressed in pajamas, leaning over his sister.

And when his eyes opened again, he saw exactly what he'd seen the moment before he left Munich.

A toilet.

16

Leila thought it was nice of Clara to pay for two rooms for her and Corey. It was not nice that the rooms shared a bathroom.

"What are you doing in there, Corey?" Leila yelled, pounding on the door. "The Sunday crossword puzzle in German?"

"*Nein*," Corey called back. "I have a . . . a really bad stomachache."

"You sound terrible. Is there anything I can do?" she asked.

"Go downstairs," he replied through the door. "There are bathrooms there. I'll meet you . . . in a minute."

Groaning with frustration, Leila ran out the apartment door and downstairs. Her stomach wasn't feeling so great either. Most of the food at the Bürgerbräukeller was grilled, fat-soaked meat, smothered in thick, gluey sauces.

By the time she went to the other bathroom and then got to Georg, it was 3:04 a.m. His hands were inside the hole he'd carved into the pillar. The wooden housing from Brög's shop sat on the floor next to him, along with a Medusa's head of tangled wires, pliers, screwdrivers, sandpaper, and a thick piece of sheepskin.

Maria and Clara were pacing next to him, looking nervously toward the door.

As Leila approached, Georg lifted the bomb, which was tucked inside its wooden housing. But as he inserted it into the pillar, it jammed.

"Brög made this housing too big," Maria explained.

Georg put his finger to his mouth to shush them both. With a worried look toward the kitchen, he wrapped a sheet of sandpaper around a wooden block the size of a large bar of soap. Holding that in one hand, he draped the sheepskin over the top and began sanding down the housing.

"Why the sheepskin?" Leila whispered.

"To make the noise not so much," Georg whispered back.

"Like a muffler," Clara explained.

"Wow," Leila said. "You really think of everything."

"I am scared," Georg said softly. "For this long time, many *Monate* . . . months? . . . no one sees me, until Corey and you. I am lucky. I like to stay lucky. Maria helps me. Clara, too. But upstairs . . ."

He pointed upward with a shudder.

Leila knew what he meant. Maria was his friend, yes. But there were many other tenants in the rooms of the Bürgerbräukeller. They were locals. In Munich, in 1939, many of them would be Nazis.

If not all.

Click.

When the door opened, Georg jolted with surprise.

"It's just Corey," Leila said.

"Sorrrrryyy," Corey whispered, tiptoeing in.

Georg pulled out his fingers, which were bloody. "*Ach.* You scare me. I sand myself."

"He's nervous," Leila explained. "And how about you? You seem to have recovered."

Corey walked straight to Georg, ignoring the question. "Can I . . . can I look at the timing mechanism?"

"*Warum?*" Georg asked. "Why?"

Corey took a deep breath. "Because Hitler is going to leave early."

"How do you know this?" Leila asked.

"I went back. I snuck back home, Leila. Just like you suggested. I did research. I had to find out."

"You did this without me?" Leila's eyes went wide. "Wait. Was *that* what you were doing in the bathroom, time-hopping on the toilet? You took the artifact and left me here? *What if something happened and I'd be stuck here without any way to get back—*"

"You have coins, right?"

"*Now you ask me?*"

"*Sssssh,*" said Georg.

Corey nodded. "He's right. The walls have ears."

Leila crossed her arms and scowled silently. *We're a team,* Corey had said. Some team. She wanted to scream at him. Time travel wasn't just about doing things on impulse. Corey may have a superpower. But he was still human. And superpowers were only as useful as the person who had them.

Corey needed Leila. He needed her planning. Her big picture way of looking at things. In the end, she hoped this scheme worked. She hoped they could go home to a better world. But no matter what happened, when this was over she would have a long talk with him.

"Georg," Corey said under his breath, kneeling next to the bomber, "you need to change the timer. That's the bottom line. Hitler is going to push everything up a half hour early. He has to get back to Berlin tomorrow. Which means he'll be taking his train at nine thirty. So he'll start at eight and cut his speech short. He's out of there at seven past nine with his Nazi posse."

"Seven minutes after nine?" Georg said. "But this is not possible. . . ."

"It happened!" Corey said. "I googled it."

He pulled out his phone, with the white charger cord still attached. Leila ran to him, putting her body between him and everyone else. "Put that thing away," she whispered through gritted teeth. "They're not ready to see something like that."

Their three older friends were staring in bafflement. "What is that in your pocket?" Clara asked.

"And what is boogled?" Maria added.

Corey held up his phone and said, "You guys took our word that we traveled in time, right? This just proves it. We call this a smartphone. Your telephones and cameras—this is where that kind of thing is going."

As they clustered around him, Corey quickly fetched

his photos. He flipped through the archival images of the Bürgerbräukeller, the bomb, and the aftermath. "Just today I hopped. I traveled back to our time. From the future, I was able to look back at what happened now. I did it because Georg asked a question I couldn't answer. If we were going to change the past—meaning, what happens tomorrow, November eighth—what was our plan? How would we know what to do if we didn't know what went wrong? I couldn't answer him then. Now I can."

Georg's eyes were wide and bloodshot. "*Das ist Zauberkunst . . .*" he murmured.

"He's saying it's magic," Leila said.

"It's technology," Corey replied. He pocketed his phone, tucking in the loop of his charger cord.

Leila watched him carefully. He didn't look good. His skin even seemed a different color, greener somehow. She thought about how little they'd slept. Maybe she didn't look so great either. Maybe this was why he was acting so weird.

Now Corey was hunkered over the bomb mechanism with Georg, Clara, and Maria. The old guy was holding it in one hand as if it were a toy.

Leila moved in for a closer look. The bomb was a collection of four metallic cylinders, wrapped tightly together with leather bands. Attached to the apparatus by a coil was a round analog clock. All of it was arranged in what looked like a homemade steel frame.

Georg twisted a knob behind the clock, making its minute and hour hands move. Sweat poured down the sides of his face, pooling on the floor. When he was done, he turned the clock face toward them. The detonation time was now set for 8:25. "Now it goes off while Hitler is giving speech," he whispered. "*Danke*, Corey. Thank you."

They all nodded silently.

Georg carefully placed the bomb back in the wooden housing. After about ten more minutes of sanding, he was finally able to push the contraption through the rectangular opening. It slid in with a scraping noise and a soft thud. "Hallelujah," Clara whispered.

Leila could hear the tick-tick-tick of the clock mechanism. It couldn't have been very loud, but it echoed insanely in the empty restaurant. As Georg shut the door of the housing, all four of them stared, intently listening.

The ticking was soft but still audible.

Georg lifted the cut-out piece of the pillar off the floor and pushed it into place, tightening it with tiny screws at the four corners. It was such a perfect, tight fit, you'd have to be right on top of it to know anything was wrong.

"Do you hear anything now?" Corey whispered.

One by one, they shook their heads no. Not even the slightest sound.

For the first time since they'd arrived, Leila saw Georg smile. He meticulously swept up the sawdust, wiped up grease stains with rags, and placed it all in his sack. When he was done, his eyes were brimming with tears. "*Viel Glück, Kinder,*" he said.

"Why," Leila said, "are you wishing us good luck? Won't you be here?"

"No, this has been Georg's plan all along," said Clara. "To set the bomb and then go into hiding. If they trace the bomb to him, it will be certain death, of course. I shall go, also. As a head of the Resistance, I will immediately be suspect. I recommend that the rest of you go, too. Corey and Leila, you may think of returning to your . . . time. The Nazis will not take kindly to the assassination of their leader."

"What?" Corey said. "No! We can't just abandon the place. What if something goes wrong?"

Clara shrugged. "It will be in God's hands. Our

work, my children, is finished."

She kissed them, one by one, on both cheeks. Then, linking arms with Georg, she began walking through the doorway that led to the kitchen. "Maria? Leila? Corey? You will join us?"

"No," Corey said. "I'm staying."

"Me, too," Leila chimed in.

"I understand," Clara said with a sigh. "Come, Maria."

Maria gave Corey and Leila an uncomfortable glance. Then she pulled a key ring from her pocket and followed Clara.

"I will let you two out," she said.

Clara blinked. "Surely you're not staying, Maria?"

"These people are working on the side of the angels," Maria replied. "I will remain with them."

17

Corey had experienced Central Park concerts where you couldn't see the grass beneath your feet. He'd been on the 42nd Street subway platform during a rush-hour train delay. He'd even managed to endure a New Year's Eve at Times Square.

But he had never seen a crowd like the one at the Bürgerbräukeller on November 8, 1939. Outside the archway, people had camped overnight to view Hitler's entrance. They were lined up Rosenheimer Street and into the center of town. All day long, people had tried to sneak onto the grounds of the restaurant. Now, close to opening time, the bridges were closed, traffic had been halted on Rosenheimer and Wiener Streets, and the din of the city had given way to a dull roar of voices, shouting, laughter, and even occasional fighting. Customers lucky enough to have gotten reservations were already inside the restaurant, drinking beer and feasting.

Corey and Leila stood at the front entrance with a bouncer named Gustav. He had a walrus-like mustache and held a thick wooden truncheon. That would have been scary enough for Corey, but it didn't seem to faze the citizens of Munich. Out of the corner of Corey's eye, he spotted three silhouettes scaling the eight-foot-high stone-and-steel fence that surrounded the restaurant grounds. As they hid behind a thicket of rosebushes that lined the restaurant, Gustav let out a soft, exasperated groan.

He muttered a stream of German to Leila, as they all headed toward the bush. "He is saying it's always the same, every year," Leila translated. "They come from all over. They drink beer like it's water. They eat like pigs. They listen to Hitler and he makes them feel good. Powerful. Then they don't pay their bills."

With a sharp swing of his truncheon, Gustav whacked the rosebush. On the other side, two teenage boys and a girl screamed and jumped out from behind. "Grrrr . . ." the guard growled, holding the wooden cylinder aloft.

As they ran off, squealing, Corey could hear the distant sound of music. It was tinny and muffled, like a brass band underwater. The din of voices from the streets grew louder. "Herr Schmuckler!" Gustav shouted into the restaurant. "*Sie kommen!*"

"*Raus! Raus!*" barked Herr Schmuckler's voice from inside. Right away, a team of waiters poured out of the restaurant, forming lines on either side of the door. Each held out an arm at ninety degrees, with a white napkin folded over the forearm. They stood with backs straight, looking out toward the archway.

Maria nodded hello to Corey and Leila as she took her place. "The insanity begins," she murmured under her breath.

As the music got louder, the crowd outside immediately quieted. Herr Schmuckler stood by the closed archway gate, waiting. In a moment the crowd began to part, clearing the road and squeezing onto the sidewalks. They fell silent, their faces growing grim.

Down the center of the street walked a small squadron of brown-suited soldiers, marching in a stiff goose step. Their boots struck the pavement together in a rhythm that didn't quite match the music. They raised their arms in an equally stiff Nazi salute, which the entire crowd returned.

Except for one man.

He was thin and middle-aged, wearing delicate wire-rim glasses and a gray tweed overcoat, standing at the curb with his chin held high. One of the soldiers noticed him immediately and barked a command in German. The man answered quietly, his arms remaining at his side.

In response the soldier removed a small wooden club from the side of his belt. But he didn't need to. Before he could raise it, the crowd fell upon the guy, fists flying and legs kicking. His glasses flew out onto the street, where they were crushed beneath the wheels of a slow-moving vehicle.

"I can't watch this," Leila said.

The resister disappeared from view as a caravan of shiny cars made its way slowly up Rosenheimer Street. Corey could hear the loud rumble of their engines over the blare of music, which blasted from loudspeakers atop one of the vehicles.

Most of the cars were roofed, but a few were convertibles, their tops down. Nazi officers, mostly older and fatter than the soldiers, saluted the crowd from their seats.

But just about everyone's eye was on a car at the rear of the procession, bigger and grander than the others. Its top was open, too, but of all the cars, it was the only one that held a man standing up.

Corey felt his mouth dry and his skin prickle. He'd seen photos of Adolf Hitler but they didn't prepare him for the flesh-and-blood version. Even blocks away, the Führer's eyes pierced the growing dusk, as if they contained a light source of their own. He was short, and much slighter than Corey had expected. His own salute seemed almost lazy, like a wave. Like he knew it really wasn't necessary to put out all the effort. And that drew all the more effort from the crowd. People seemed to be trying to touch him, their faces strained and tear streaked.

The cars puttered through the archway, and then they parked along the inner drive. Outside the restaurant, Herr Schmuckler, Gustav, Maria, and all the staff returned the Nazi salute. Corey stared in disbelief.

He felt a jab in his rib cage. "Salute!" Leila hissed. "You saw what they did to that guy!"

She was raising her hand, too. Corey felt sick to his stomach even thinking about it. But he knew she was right, and he forced his arm upward.

Herr Schmuckler greeted Hitler and an entourage of about ten other Nazi officers. Corey recognized some of them from his research—Himmler, Göring, some of the most barbaric murderers in history. None of them seemed to want to chitchat with Schmuckler, who was jabbering away about the menu.

As Hitler passed, he stopped and turned. Corey expected him to look back and wave to his fans. But his eyes caught Corey's, and his expression twisted into a bizarre, almost clownish smile. Up close, the bags under his eyes were like elephant skin, his cheeks hollow and sad. The intensity of his gaze seemed to slice Corey's face in half, and he couldn't help but flinch. *"Wie geht's, mein Junge?"* Hitler said in a voice that was shockingly high-pitched and soft. *"Haben wir uns schon kennengelernt?"*

Corey kept an ear open for Leila to translate. She had to swallow several times before saying, "He wants to know if you've met before."

"No!" Corey blurted.

"Ah, *Amerikanisch!*" Hitler said.

Behind Hitler, journalists were taking photos with cameras the size of small SUVs. Each photo came with a blinding light and a sound like a muffled explosion. Corey realized he'd put his saluting arm down, so he raised it again. At the same moment Hitler shifted his weight, and Corey's hand nearly hit him in the face.

The Führer had to move aside, and a gasp went through the gathering.

One of Hitler's henchmen rushed toward Corey. He was skinny and blond, with a moonscape of pimples on either side of a sharp nose. He grabbed Corey's other arm and began to pull him forward. *"Was machst du, junge Straftäter?"*

"He's not a delinquent!" Leila blurted. "It was a mistake! *Zufällig!*"

Behind the soldier, Hitler let out a sharp, barking laugh. He shook his head with merriment and stomped a foot on the floor. "Haaaaa hahaha! *Ja, ja, lass ihn los,* Bruno! *Er hat mich mit seiner enthusiastischen Loyalität fast getötet!*"

Hitler's people were chuckling now, and the Führer turned to wink at them. And Leila leaned toward Corey, quickly whispering, "He said, 'Yes, yes, leave him, Bruno. He almost killed me with his enthusiastic loyalty!'"

Now all the other, sober-faced older officers echoed Hitler's laughter. Obediently, the Bürgerbräukeller staff joined in, too. Bruno the sharp-nosed soldier, whose face was already a deep shade of pink, reddened with anger. Corey could tell he did not enjoy the mockery.

"They're laughing with you, not at you," Corey said.

Bruno stepped aside obediently as Hitler reached toward Corey. The Führer clapped his hand fondly around the back of Corey's neck, smiling for the cameras. Then, letting go, he turned and headed into the restaurant.

When Hitler's back was turned, Bruno pulled Corey close so they were nose to nose. Corey could feel the heat from the guy's face and smell cigarettes and salami on his breath. *"Vorsichtig, Schweinchen. Ich passe auf dich auf,"* he hissed. *"Wir treffen uns wieder drin."*

He shoved Corey away so hard he nearly fell over, then marched back into the entourage.

"What did he say?" Corey asked.

Leila swallowed hard. "'Be careful, piglet. I have my eyes on you. We will meet again inside.'"

18

Corey's knees were shaking as he and Leila entered the Bürgerbräukeller.

"I. Can't. Even," Leila said.

"Me neither," Corey replied.

"That was Adolf Hitler," Leila said. "He put a hand on you. What was going through your mind?"

"You want to know the truth? I wanted a selfie. Because no one will ever believe me."

"That is revolting!"

"I know."

As Hitler descended the staircase, a roar went up from the crowd. The room had been crammed with maybe twice as many tables as usual, and every seat was already taken. In the balconies, people rushed to the railings to see. An aisle had been left down the middle of the main floor, and as Hitler marched to the stage, everyone stood. Someone cried "Heil, Hitler!" and the room erupted into a deafening chant as the Führer mounted the two steps to the stage.

Corey looked at the clock on the wall. Georg had synchronized it to match the bomb's clock to the second.

8:02.

Twenty-three minutes before the explosion.

"Remember," Leila said, "at eight fifteen we leave this dump."

The Nazi officers sat in chairs behind Hitler. He stood at the podium, just a foot or so from the pillar. Maria had managed to get the staff of the Bürgerbräukeller to move the tables away from the bomb. The customers were Nazi sympathizers, but the point was to get Hitler, not cause collateral damage.

But now the people in front, eager to be closer, were sliding their tables toward Hitler's podium. Maria rushed over, trying to smile and sweet-talk the people into moving back. The last thing she wanted to do was arouse suspicion. "She's telling them they're too close to the Führer and he needs breathing room," Leila said to Corey.

"She's putting herself in danger," Corey said.

Hitler watched the commotion with mild impatience. He took the opportunity to snap a vigorous Nazi salute to the crowd, which everyone returned.

Corey scanned the faces. The most chilling thing to him was that they didn't look angry or evil or brainwashed. They looked happy. If you'd shown Corey a photo of their faces, minus the salute, he would have thought they were watching Olympic skating or a dog show. "This is making me sick," he said.

The moment Hitler began, the crowd dropped back into their seats and fell instantly quiet, like someone had turned a switch. Hitler began to speak in a forceful but low voice. The people hung on every word, leaving entire meals untouched on their plates. Even the waiters, who had been scurrying from table to table, stood transfixed. "What's he saying?" Corey asked.

"'The German people are emerging from the dark into a new . . . glory'?" Leila said. "Stuff like that, over and over."

Hitler was picking up steam now, gesturing with his hands, pounding his fists.

"Okay, now he's saying that true Germans have been robbed," Leila continued. "By a small group of greedy invaders that go by the name . . ."

She didn't finish, but Corey knew. The last word in Hitler's sentence was *"Juden!"*

The people stood again. Now their faces were twisted and resentful. They were cupping their hands to their mouths, shouting back to the stage. Hitler tipped his chin up, looking from side to side with hands on hips.

The clock said 8:11.

As a chant of *Sieg heil* broke out, people began rushing forward. Hitler continued, his voice rising in pitch and volume until he was practically shouting. His movements became jerky and odd, his greasy hair flying across his forehead, his eyes bugging out. Half of Corey wanted to burst out giggling, but the horrified half kept him quiet.

More than anything else, he wanted an image of this. If his mission was going to be successful, he wanted a reminder of what he'd seen.

With all eyes focused on the stage, Corey angled his body away from facing Leila. He pulled his phone from his pocket. It was still connected to the cord, but he left it that way. He had to do this fast.

Making sure no one was looking, he cupped the phone in both hands, hiding it from sight, his thumbs poised over the screen. He lifted his hands to his face as if he were about to sneeze, making sure the lens was unobstructed. The white cord hung down, but it didn't matter. He could have stripped naked and danced, and no one would have noticed. As he got the image of Hitler on his screen, he snapped a couple of photos. Quickly he scrolled through them to make sure they were okay. Picture one was too dark, but pictures two, three, and four were amazing. The fifth photo was the image of the bomb he'd saved from his web search when he was in the present, so he shut the phone off and slipped it back into his pocket.

There was a commotion in the front now. People had left their tables and were squeezing into the space Maria had cleared, the buffer zone between the tables and Hitler. They were staring adoringly at the Führer, directly in front of the podium. Maria was trying to herd them away, back to their tables. She was whispering, trying not to disturb the speech. Hitler didn't even seem to notice her. But his officers, sitting behind him, were scowling.

"She's trying to save those people's lives," Corey said.

"Why is she doing that?" Leila asked. "They're Nazis!"

"We have to help her."

"We have to leave in four minutes!"

"Maria is right in front of the bomb, Leila!"

Together they raced up the aisle toward the stage. "*Maria, pass auf!*" Leila yelled.

A few people turned, looking annoyed. But most looked to be in a state of hypnosis. Hitler looked over their heads, shouting and gesticulating as if nothing unusual were happening.

The clock said 8:14.

Eleven more minutes.

Corey and Leila grabbed Maria's arms and pulled her away from the podium. Onstage, Bruno's eyes pinned Corey. The young officer slipped away from his seat, circled back into the shadows, and then ran toward Corey. Grabbing him by the arm, he pulled him away from the stage. He shoved Corey down a path between the tables, in the direction of the kitchen.

"Get your hands off him!" Leila shouted.

She caught up with them at the restaurant wall, not far from the kitchen. Grabbing the young Nazi's arm, she yanked him away.

As Bruno lurched back, caught off guard, his fingers caught on something sticking out of Corey's pocket.

The white charger cord.

With a sinking stomach, Corey realized he hadn't

shoved the cord fully in after taking the photos. And because the wire was still attached to his phone, Bruno's grab had pulled it halfway out of his pocket.

"Oh. Sorry. That's mine," Corey said.

Bruno locked eyes with Corey and sneered. "We meet again, American dog," he said in a heavy accent, grabbing the phone. "And what is this? A weapon?"

"You speak English?" Corey said.

"No-o-o-o!" Leila cried out.

"*Sssshhhhh!*" shushed a well-dressed couple at a nearby table.

Hitler bellowed on, reaching some kind of climax. Now people were jumping to their feet. But Bruno was transfixed by the smartphone. He tapped it, nearly shrieking as it lit up. Corey's screen showed a ticking analog clock, set to New York time. Bruno's eyes followed the white cord right into Corey's pocket. "*Lieber Gott . . .*" he murmured. "*Ist es möglich?*"

"It's a long story," Corey said, trying to grab the phone back. "Look, it's a phone, that's all."

His thumb grazed the Home button, which sensed his print and caused the start screen to vanish. In its place was the last image Corey had seen before putting the phone away.

The screen grab of Georg's bomb.

"*Eine Bombe?*" Bruno muttered. "*Eine kleine Bombe?*"

"He thinks your phone is a small bomb," Leila said. "Or a detonator, or something."

Corey grabbed the phone back. "It's just a picture. Look. You want to see more?"

But Bruno was sprinting back toward the stage. "*Es ist eine Bombe!*"

The other officers leaped to their feet. Now Hitler had noticed. His face went pale, his eyes trained on Corey like a death ray.

Now Maria was rushing toward them. "Tell them it's harmless!" Corey said.

"*Nein! Es ist keine Bombe!*" Maria shouted back toward the stage. "*Es ist harmlos!*"

Bruno leaped toward Hitler, shielding him with his body. Behind Corey, the room was slow to react. But as the word *Bombe* made its way through the crowd, people began stampeding for the stairway.

"Stay!" Corey said to the group of Nazis, holding out his phone. "It's a telephone. Telephone! It has pictures!"

Corey felt a firm hand on his shoulder. "Corey, come on! This thing is going to blow!"

Instead of heading for the staircase, Leila pulled Corey toward the door at the back of the stage area.

With Maria, they sped down the hallway toward the kitchen. From behind them came the tromping footsteps of other restaurant workers.

As they reached the kitchen, a team of dishwashers looked at them as if they'd lost their minds.

"Corey, we have to get out of here, now!" Leila said.

Corey yanked the backpack off his shoulders and reached inside, just as the clock clicked to 8:25.

19

Normally Corey liked snow. But he preferred it fluffy and soft and under his feet. Not wet and icy and in his face.

"What just happened?" Leila asked. "Corey, did the bomb go off?"

"Pkaacchh." Corey spat out the snow and sat up, in a mound of slush on the side of an icy river. He was happy to hear Leila's voice, because he couldn't see much. His head felt swollen, making his vision blurry. Above them the sky was gray and greasy-looking, tinged orange by streetlights barely visible though the fog. The temperature had dropped about twenty degrees. The night was quiet save for the laughing of distant voices, the putter of a car engine, and the clopping of horse hooves. "I don't know. I guess so. It feels like we got blown out of the restaurant."

Leila stood. "Through the roof of the kitchen and clear across town to the Isar River? Where five inches of snow fell in a sudden furious blizzard that we didn't notice?"

"Yeah, good point." Corey blinked and took a few deep wintry breaths. He could see more now. They were on the broad bank of a broad river. To their left, at the base of an ornate stone bridge, a homeless man slept curled in a blanket. Each stanchion of the bridge held a lamp with a flaming torch. A soot-faced man in a dark suit was adjusting one of the flames, but he paused to tip his hat to another man crossing the bridge on horseback. "This doesn't feel like nineteen thirty-nine," Corey said. "I think we hopped backward."

"Duh," Leila reacted. "But how?"

"I reached into my backpack, Leila," Corey said. "We have artifacts in there. I wanted to get us out—"

"But we were in the kitchen!" Leila protested. "We were far enough from the bomb. We wouldn't have been affected."

"You wanted to stay?" Corey said.

"Yes! Now we don't know what happened! Did Hitler escape in time? Did we get him?"

Corey groaned with the effort of standing up. The last few hours were running in his mind, in all their nightmarish detail. "I messed up. We failed, Leila. Hitler survived."

"How can you be so sure?"

"He and his people were racing out of the place way before the bomb was set to blow," Corey said. "They were gone by the time we were at the door at the back of that stage."

"But the bomb could have collapsed the place—"

"In all those archival photos I saw back in New York? The only damaged part of the restaurant was under that balcony, remember? He was far from that. And it's all my fault. Because I was too careless about my phone. It would have worked if that guy hadn't seen my cord."

"Yeah, but we changed history, remember? We changed the timing of the bomb—"

"I changed history."

"Right. So anything could have happened." Leila stood up, too. She exhaled a white puff of breath and shuddered. "I'm dying to know."

Corey was already checking his phone. "No cell service."

"What a surprise."

In the fog it was hard to see very far. On the other side of the bridge, torchlit paths wandered through what looked like a park setting. On this side, people were streaming out of a grand brightly lit building ornamented with statues of cherubs and bare-chested Greek gods. The locals strolled arm in arm down a set of stairs, the women in furs and the men in top hats and long wool coats. Some were met at the curb by horse-drawn coaches and some by drivers in shining old-style cars.

"Model Ts . . ." Corey murmured.

Leila drew her arms around herself and shivered. "Where are we?"

Corey reached into his pack and pulled out the framed painting by Leila's great-uncle. "I must have touched this."

Leila's face brightened. "Vienna, nineteen oh eight," she said. "This is where I wanted us to go in the first place. It's where Opa's dad went to school—"

"The Vienna Academy of Fine Arts," Corey said.

"Exactly!"

From the street came a loud voice attempting some kind of song. "*We-e-e-r hat so viel Pinke-Pinke . . . we-e-e-er hat so viel Ge-e-e-eld?*"

Two men were staggering off the sidewalk toward

Corey and Leila. The snow was throwing them both off-balance, so they put their arms around each other's shoulders for support. One of them, a broad, blue-eyed young guy with a cleft chin and bright red hair, held up a half-empty bottle and shouted *"Guten Morgen!"* This made the other guy burst out laughing. He was thin, dark, and dressed in black, with straight black hair that jutted out the sides of a knit cap.

"What's so funny?" Corey said.

"He said 'Good morning,'" Leila replied.

"And it's night," Corey said dryly. "I get it. Hilarious."

The guys approached them on rubbery legs. *"Geld für Überlebenskünstler?"* asked Blue Eyes. *"Oder vielleicht ein Kuss?"*

"Hau ab!" Leila said.

She and Corey backed away. "He asked if we have money for a starving artist. Or maybe a kiss. I told him to get lost."

"Ew," Corey said. "He doesn't look starving anyway. He looks drunk."

But Corey's eyes were trained on Mr. Black Hair. He was thin and sensitive looking, with high cheekbones, piercing eyes, and a mole on his left cheek. Corey tried to imagine him with the hat off, thirty years older and heavier. He pictured bags under the guy's eyes and a brown Nazi suit. "Leila," he whispered, "do you think that's him—the black-haired guy?"

"Who?"

"The Führer who must not be named!" Corey said. "He'd be about eighteen now."

"No way. This guy is too handsome."

The big guy let out a huge belch. He wasn't looking at them anymore, but farther up the riverbank. Leila's retort seemed to make him lose interest. Now he began dragging Black Hair toward the man who was sleeping by the bridge abutment. "Aaahh. Hahahaha!" he cackled. "*Ein schlafender Hund.*"

"He just called that guy a sleeping dog," Leila whispered.

"Wow. Super clever insults," Corey said. "He could go into politics."

The two guys stumbled toward the unsuspecting man. Blue Eyes seemed to find him hilarious. "*Arf, arf!*" he barked. "*Wachen Sie auf! Schon Zeit zu arbeiten, Sie Faulpelz!*"

"'Wake up! It's time to go to work, lazybones!'" Leila translated.

"Jackass bully," Corey murmured.

The homeless guy didn't answer and didn't move. "He looks dead," Leila said.

"Arf, arf!" Blue Eyes repeated.

Black Hair began pulling him away. "Otto, *komm.*"

Instead the red-haired man, Otto, yanked himself free. With a grunt, he stepped toward the homeless man and delivered a sharp soccer kick to his side.

The guy cried out in agony. He struggled to his feet. Even tangled in his thick, tattered blanket, he was obviously small and skinny and no match for Otto.

His reaction made the bully howl with laughter. *"Tanzen Sie, Teufel, tanzen Sie!"* he yelled, as Black Hair tried again to pull him away.

"'Dance, devil, dance,'" Leila translated.

"He can't do this," Corey said. "Come on, there's strength in numbers."

They both rushed through the snow toward the mounting fight. The old painting from Leila's great-grandfather slipped out of Corey's hand into the snow. But he couldn't think about that now.

The homeless guy's face caught the light. It was bony and hollow and sad, lined with soot. His eyes were wide with fear, his nose small and delicate. He muttered something that Corey couldn't hear, but it made Otto scream with rage.

The big guy lurched toward the poor man, who leaped aside with the grace of someone who had not been drinking. He grabbed a rock from the ground and held it aloft.

"Otto!" screamed Black Hair, trying once again to pull his bigger friend away.

Otto, still a little unsteady on his legs, looked down at his feet as if he'd stepped on something.

He had—a branch. He dug it out of the snow and held it with two arms like a baseball bat. Otto and the homeless man circled each other warily, each lurching forward to threaten the other. Then, with a roar, Otto took a vicious swing at the homeless guy.

At the last moment the ragged man jumped away. The swing missed, and it spun Otto around. Planting his feet, the poor man reared back to throw the rock at Otto. But it was too heavy and the effort made him lose his balance. As he plopped down into the snow, the rock arced through the air and smacked Otto in the ankle.

Otto grimaced, gritting his teeth with pain. With a deep, angry cry, he charged forward. Steadying him-self by the helpless man, he raised the branch high and brought it down toward the man's head.

20

Corey didn't know he could move so fast.

And after he did, he wasn't sure he ever wanted to do it again.

He landed facedown on the homeless guy, his stomach directly over the man's face. He felt the branch strike him across the back, exactly where the guy's head would have been.

For a moment, Corey's body took the shock of the blow. Then the pain spread like an explosion from head to toe. "*Yeeeeoowwww!*" Corey screamed, rolling onto the snow.

Leila and Black Hair were all over Otto now, wrestling him to the ground. He seemed just as shocked at his own actions as Corey was.

"*Dummkopf! Barbar! Unmensch!*" Black Hair screamed, pulling on Otto's curly red hair.

Otto's eyes welled up. He looked confused and angry and sorry, all at the same time. As if he'd just awoken from a dream. He pleaded with Black Hair in German.

"Corey, are you okay?" Leila shouted, running toward him.

Corey stood. He couldn't straighten out. He could barely open his eyes. "It's only a flesh wound."

The homeless guy leaped to his feet, linking a supportive arm into Corey's. "*Danke,*" he said. "*Du hast mein Leben gerettet.*"

"You're . . . welcome . . . I think . . ." Corey replied through gritted teeth.

But the homeless man was wasting no time near Otto. Eyeing his attacker fearfully, he scampered away. In a moment he disappeared along the shadows of the bridge. Otto leaped up. "*Ich weiß nicht was passiert ist,*" he said, then bolted after the man. "*Moment mal! Es tut mir leid. Es tut mir leid!*"

"He's trying to apologize," Leila explained.

"*Ach . . .*" With an exasperated shake of the head, the black-haired guy dismissively waved toward his friend.

"You saved that homeless man's life, Corey," Leila

said. "That's what he said to you."

"Maybe . . . he can bring me some ice cream . . ." Corey rasped. "That always helps extreme pain."

"Please, I am sorry," the man with the black hair piped up. "Is that the right word *auf Englisch*, 'sorry'?"

"Yes," Leila said. "But it wasn't your fault."

"It was," he replied. "I am sorry for Otto. He is very gentle man, inside. He is watercolor painter at Academy. Is hard to believe. But when drunk? He is . . . what is word? Monster. He has with many people make fight. So I take him home. For sleep. We walk and we talk along *die Donau* . . . Danube. Then we see you. Otto is thinking *ihre Kleidung* . . . clothing . . . is . . . what is the word *auf Englisch*? . . . *ungewöhnlich*?"

"Unusual. You think our clothing is unusual?" Leila burst out laughing. "From nineteen thirty-nine? You would love Corey's sneakers."

"*Wie bitte?* Nineteen thirty-nine?" the man said.

"Never mind," Leila replied. "You were saying?"

"Ah, yes. We are walking, and Otto says he wants to marry you. He pulls me to meet you. You see? If he does not pull me, we do not see sleeping man. So I apologize."

"I don't think it's good to be friends with someone who attacks random guys for no reason," Corey said.

"Or says he wants to marry total strangers," Leila added. "He's kind of a pig."

"Yes, you are right." The man shook his head. "Otto knows this man by the bridge. Does not like him. This man . . . he sells art on streets. Art painted by famous artists. For high money. But is not really the artist work."

"Wait. The homeless guy sells bootleg art?" Corey said.

"Boot leg? No, is mostly landscape . . . still life. You? You are artist too? Visiting from America?"

"Visitors, yes," Leila said. "I'm Leila."

"I'm Corey." As Corey stuck out his hand, he winced. Every movement hurt.

The man smiled sympathetically as he shook Corey's hand. "You are in pain."

"Only when I breathe," Corey said through a grimace.

"I will take you to Academy hospital," the man said.

Leila gave Corey a nervous glance. "We . . . don't really have a lot of money."

"Like, zero," Corey said. "But I appreciate it. We're actually here looking for someone? Maybe you can help?"

"Of course I will help," he said. "But please to not

worry with hospital. Tomorrow your pain will be very, very bad. I—my family—will pay."

"What? Really?" Leila said. "Who are you?"

"Ach, so sorry!" The man blushed, holding out his hand. "I am Fritzie. Fritzie Scharfstein."

Leila, who was standing, fell flat down onto her rear end. "Oh . . . dear . . . lord . . . I feel weak."

Fritzie smiled curiously. "Perhaps you need to go to the hospital, too."

The next morning Corey awoke at 9:00. He was instantly aware that his eyelids were the only part of his body that didn't feel like it was in a meat grinder.

"Owwww!" he groaned.

"Good morning to you, too." Leila was standing next to his bed, clutching a bouquet of flowers. "These smell nice."

"I can't tell," Corey replied. "My nose hurts."

"He's such a nice guy," Leila said. "So charming."

"*Who?*" Corey asked.

"My great-grandfather Fritzie. He's just like Opa." Leila unwrapped the flowers and put them in a glass vase by a window. They were in a long room with a high ceiling and a wood floor. The walls were lined with beds. Next to Corey was a sleeping man with his leg in traction. A moaning young woman with green-ish skin lay next to him, and a man with a patched eye was patiently reading a book in the bed near her. Official-looking men and women in bad-fitting clothes bustled about from bed to bed, giving advice and answering questions. There wasn't an IV drip or a single beeping gauge anywhere to be seen. "Did anybody actually get better in places like this?" Corey groaned.

"Fritzie let me stay in the apartment of a friend who was traveling," Leila said. "We walked here together. On the way we passed a flower shop that wasn't even open. He knocked on the door and got someone to put together this bouquet. When he got here, he convinced the staff that you and I were his visiting younger sib-lings. Isn't that sweet?"

"You and I don't look anything alike," Corey said.

"But he and I do," Leila said, "even though the hair is different. Security in nineteen oh eight isn't like it is today. The doctor says you just have a very bad bruise. No broken bones. It's going to take a while. He's going to let you out today with some kind of back brace. We're having lunch with Fritzie at a fancy café. You got lucky."

"I don't feel lucky. I think I need an MRI. But I guess I'll have to wait a century."

From down the hall, a nurse summoned Leila. "Excuse me," Leila said.

As she jogged away, Corey piled pillows behind his back and sat up. The view outside the window made the pain go away a little.

Last night's fog had cleared, and the hospital over-looked a sun-drenched square. The sound of horse hooves punctuated a constant whoosh of falling water from an exuberant fountain. The buildings shone, whitewashed and sparkling clean. Just about every structure was intricately ornamented. Winged babies peeked out from roofs, and entire walls were made of stones carved with deeply shadowed curlicues. People on foot clogged the roads, not a stoplight in sight. An occasional black car bounced clumsily by, swerving to avoid contact with pedestrians. A steady stream of horse-drawn carriages moved in either direction. No one seemed to be in too much of a hurry, save for an occasional bearded man in a three-piece suit, checking a pocket watch.

"Corey?" Leila said. "We have a visitor."

With a smile, she gestured behind her. A skinny young guy, carrying a shoulder bag and clothed in a shabby suit several sizes too big, shuffled into the room. He was wearing a beret, which he removed as he got close to the bed. "*Guten Morgen*," he said.

Corey smiled. It was the homeless guy from the night before.

"I know what that means," Corey replied. "Good morning to you."

His eyes were blue, his face gaunt. His hair looked like it could use a shampoo and maybe some insect repellent. He smiled brightly at Corey and shifted his shoulder bag. "I bring gift," he said softly. "For saving my life."

Corey smiled. Last night, under the bridge, this guy had seemed smaller and meeker. Cleaned up, he looked more confident. There was something weirdly familiar about his voice, but by now most German-accented English sounded alike to Corey.

"How did you find us?" Leila asked.

"I am poor," he said. "I live in the street. I see where everyone goes." With a proud flourish, he took a framed painting from his bag. It was pretty much the scene outside the hospital window—a bright city square with the Alps rising majestically in the background. The details were accurate, the colors vibrant.

"That's really good!" Leila said. "Thank you."

"Vienna is great perspiration!" the man said. "Great schools. Many great artists and beautiful mountains! The Ring Road, the Opera House, the Parliament!"

"Inspiration," Corey corrected him. He reached for the painting, wondering what in the world he and Leila were going to do with this.

The man smiled. "I sell paintings. Postcards. But so many artists here! So many talent! Many people see my art, they make joking. They say I am not good."

"You are good," Corey said. "You have to keep trying."

"*Danke*," the man said, bowing his head modestly. "I try a long time. But now I do not have mark for a home. I lose . . . *Hoffnung*."

"Hope," Leila translated.

"*Ja*," the man said. "Yesterday I am afraid it is all *fertig*. Over for me. I did not expect such kindness from a savior like you!"

"That is so sweet," Leila said. "Sorry it's been hard for you. But Corey's right. You're talented."

"You will see," the man said. "I will be great artist some day. This painting will be worth many money. Will make you rich. Rich like the *Juden*. I will move to Alps and paint until I am old man. You like?"

Corey tried to answer, but no words came. He was

staring at the signature at the bottom of the painting. "This is your name?"

The man's brow furrowed. "*Ja.*"

As Leila came closer, Corey tilted the painting so she could see the writing.

A. HITLER

21

"We saved his life," Corey said in disbelief, limping down the sidewalk from the hospital.

"Corey . . ." Leila said.

"We had a chance to get him in nineteen thirty-nine—when he'd already done damage to the world!" Corey thundered. "And now? Now, when all I have to do is sit back and let someone else club him over the head, way before Der Creepo has even dreamed of politics, what do I do? *I save his life and kill my back instead!*"

"You didn't know," Leila reminded him.

"I *should* have known," Corey said. "The eyes. That voice. Did you hear what he said about the *Juden?*"

"He looks a lot different without the paintbrush mustache."

Corey whirled around to her. His back brace took some of the pain away, but his anger took away the rest. "This guy will grow up to order mass murder. Already you can see it. The *Juden* have all the money, that's what he said. Now he's all boo-hoo-I'm-so-depressed. But soon it will be I-am-invincible! And one of those people he'll murder will be Fritzie. We saved Hitler's life and killed your great-grandfather!"

"Look, I know you're mad at yourself and your back hurts, but calm down." Leila's face was growing red. Her eyes teared up, and when she spoke her jaw trembled. "I could get mad at you, too, Corey. You were the one who wanted to save Maria. If we'd just left, the bomb would have gone off. But you're human. I know that. I'm human, too. And I just met my great-grandfather. Fritzie's not just a story now. He's not just some tragic figure the family talks about. He's flesh and blood. Alive and young and talented. He's full of optimism and I know he's going to die in the worst way. Look, we're still here, and we're not done. We've been given another chance to finish the job. So I will not let you beat yourself up about what happened."

"Sorry," Corey said, starting to walk again. "You're right. I'm cranky. Everything hurts."

He sat at the edge of the fountain. It was past rush hour but not lunchtime yet, and the square was pretty empty. A small crowd had gathered at the entrance to one of the buildings. Their backs were to Corey and Leila as they stared at a sign advertising "Kunstschau Wien 1908," with a huge abstract image that looked like a man and woman kissing.

Looking right and left, Corey pulled the phone from his pocket. There was very little charge left. Quickly he navigated to the Hitler biography he had downloaded. "Okay, look, we need to learn about this guy. This bio has a lot about his time here. In nineteen oh eight, Vienna was like the center of the world for culture. Famous artists, musicians, architects, thinkers, they flocked here. Here—there's even an image of that huge painting those people are looking at. It's called *The Kiss*, by a guy named Klimt. He's part of this movement called Vienna Secession. Their art was abstract and modern, more like design and less like realism. It was controversial and shocking. But I don't know what they were seceding from." He gave Leila a look. "Seceding means withdrawing, right?"

"Seceding from the fancy old style, I guess," Leila

said. "Look around. The architecture is so old-world classical. It's like one big grandparents' fantasy village."

"All kinds of other new things were being discovered here," Corey said. "Freud lived in Vienna. He put people on the couch for the first time. Called it the talking cure and made all kinds of breakthroughs in mental health."

"Maybe we should send Hitler to him," Leila suggested.

"Like you said, he's not *Hitler* Hitler yet," Corey said, scrolling through the bio. "In nineteen oh eight he's just one of the many starving artists here in Vienna."

"A starving artist who hates Jews."

"Sometimes he's living in homeless shelters, sometimes on the streets. Even though there are all these rich people going to galleries and concerts, there's a lot of poverty here. The suicide rate is really high."

Leila looked around. "It just seems so . . . prosperous, and peaceful."

"Okay, check this out." Corey began reading aloud. "'The young Adolf came to Vienna with a letter of introduction to a graphic artist and stage designer, the famously loud and egotistical Alfred Roller. At the time Roller was the head designer of the Vienna Court Opera, one of the most prestigious positions in the cultural world. The letter was designed to gain Hitler an apprenticeship, in the hopes he would develop his skills and eventually become a successful artist. But the young Hitler could not bring himself to meet Roller. Three times he went to the studio, vowing to knock on the door. In his autobiography, Hitler confesses that on his third and last visit, his knuckles were poised to strike, yet he turned away and later burned the letter, never to return. In nineteen oh nine he applied to the Vienna Academy of Fine Arts. But now he was competing with future world-class artists, relying only on his own modest merits. He was rejected. Later in life Hitler claimed that this was the best thing to happen to him; it pushed him into politics.'"

Leila stared at the screen. "So . . . if he *had* apprenticed with that guy, Roller . . ."

Corey nodded. "The history of the world would have been so different."

"Wow . . . because of a few inches between a knuckle and a door," Leila said. "I wonder if he's done it yet?"

"Done what?"

"Burned the letter! Maybe he hasn't gone to Roller's place for the third time. Or even the first or second."

Pocketing his phone, Corey jumped off the fountain

ledge. As his feet hit the pavement, his entire aching body screamed in revolt. "Owwww! Remind me never to do that again. I feel like I'm a hundred and three."

"Easy, Grandpa," Leila said. "Where are we going?"

"To change the world," he said. "First we meet Fritzie at the café. And then we ask him to take us to Adolf Hitler."

22

Café Central was on a corner where two narrow streets met. One of them was called Herrengasse, which sounded to Corey like the word for an aquatic bird fart. Even before lunch hour, the sidewalk seats were nearly full, despite the chill in the air. People sipped espresso and ate pastries and little cubed sandwiches. They spoke in German, French, English, and languages Corey couldn't recognize. The café had tall, vaulted windows. Through them Corey could see a cozy space of polished dark wood walls and marble tables. The sound of a tinkling piano spilled onto the sidewalk. As they entered, the smell of coffee and sweets made Corey drool.

"I'm nervous," Leila said, clutching Corey's arm.

"Hi, nervous. I'm hungry," Corey replied.

"We're standing here, about to meet Fritzie, and all I want to do is cry," Leila said, "because I know his future. He's such a nice man. He's kind and talented and chill and a little goofy. He's going to be all smiley and confident, and all I want to do is tell him to escape, go to America now, *do something*. But if I say that, he'll think I'm a lunatic. And if I don't . . ." Her voice trailed off.

"If you don't, *what*?" Corey said.

"I'm the one who's supposed to be positive. Glass half full. But how can I face him? How can I smile and tell jokes, knowing what happened to him?" Leila exhaled. "How do you even think straight when you're doing this?"

Corey put his arm around her. "Hey, it didn't happen yet. It's nineteen oh eight. I can do this."

"We," Leila reminded him.

"We," Corey repeated. "We're going to get Hitler to the big-shot designer guy at the opera. And then I'm going to change the course of history, with no violence."

"First I have to cheer you up, then you do the same for me. This is hard."

"Time travel is not for wusses," Corey said.

They went into the restaurant. Fritzie was sitting at an upright piano just inside the café. He wore a brimmed hat cocked to one side and a slightly raggedy scarf. His fingers flew over the keyboard. But it wasn't a classical piece like the one they'd heard on the vinyl record in New York, at Leila's apartment. It was a jazzy, bouncy tune with a pounding rhythm that was making customers get up from their seats and dance. He was grunting along to the tune, just the way they'd heard him in the old recording, back home.

Corey and Leila waited until he stopped, which he did with a big, dramatic flourish. As they joined in a loud burst of cheering, he spun around and saw them. "Ah, here are the Americans!" he said.

That led to another round of applause.

Leila was blushing. "We didn't do anything."

"You brought us ragtime!" Fritzie said with a big smile. "Your brilliant Mr. Scott Joplin. You know this music?"

"No," Corey said.

"Yes," Leila piped up. "And you're amazing!"

"Thank you! You see, this is how I make money for my studies. Last week I perform at the school. Brahms, Beethoven, Bach. Tonight I play for important people at the opera house." Fritzie's face brightened, and he took

Leila by the arm. "You come? Please! Is party. I will put you on the list. I play classical, too!"

"Uh, sure," Leila said.

As Fritzie leaped up from the piano, Leila impulsively threw her arms around him. "Oh, Fritzie, thanks for everything you've done for us—the hospital, the lodging. . . ."

He laughed and returned the embrace. "It is my pleasure. And you, Corey, are you feeling better?"

Corey backed stiffly away. "I am, if you don't hug me."

They wandered out to one of the tables on Herrengasse, where Fritzie ordered from the waiter in German. "All of Vienna passes the Café Central," Fritzie said. "We sit and eat and see famous people. Maybe Freud, Trotsky, Schiele. I will pay."

Corey angled his seat out toward the street. All along Herrengasse, artists had set up easels and were selling paintings and postcards. Some of them were dressed in paint-spattered smocks, some were chanting to attract attention. "That poor man Otto almost killed yesterday?" Corey said. "Does he come here?"

"Adolf?" Fritzie said. "*Manchmal.* Sometimes. He does not get here early enough, maybe. This man, he is not very . . . how do you say . . . *aggressiv?*"

Corey could see Leila shudder.

The two of them lapsed into German. Fritzie spoke very fast, which made Leila giggle and ask him to slow down. But they settled into a rhythm, and it made Corey happy to see them bond.

Normally Corey didn't drink coffee, and he winced when the waiter plopped a cappuccino down in front of him along with a croissant. But after a couple of sips, he liked the combination of the sweetness of cinnamon, the smoothness of warm milk, and the slight bitterness of coffee.

On the fourth sip, he nearly choked.

That was when a short man with comically quick, bouncing steps sped by on Herrengasse. His hair flapped up and down in the breeze. Even though he carried a big sack over his shoulder, he was so slight and shabby that people didn't move an inch for him, as if he were invisible.

But there was no mistaking the face of the man they met in the hospital, Adolf Hitler.

Corey elbowed Leila. "There he goes."

He sprang from his seat, making sure to shove the croissant in his pocket. The pain in his back nearly smacked him down, but he forced himself to move. Staying to the walls, Corey threaded through the people toward the center of town, following the odd gait of Hitler. He finally lost Hitler in a crowd of people at an open square in front of a stately columned building. There he stopped, frantically looking around.

"Corey!" Leila's voice called out from behind him. She came running up and took Corey's arm. "Where is he?"

"I don't know," Corey replied.

Leila glanced around too. "I told Fritzie you ran off because you were freaked out by the sight of a rat."

"True, kind of. He believed it?"

"I think he thinks Americans are strange. So yeah."

"*There!*" Corey said, spotting a familiar blotch of greasy black hair in the crowd. Hitler was standing near the front, facing the steps of the building. From the front door, a bearded man emerged, clasping his hands together in front of his tweed suit and smiling at the crowd.

As they responded with loud cheers, Corey and Leila made their way toward the front. "*Entschuldigung, bitte . . . Entschuldigung . . .*" Leila repeated. Excuse me, excuse me.

The man descended the steps slowly. He waved at individuals he spotted in the throng. His beard was full and fluffy, a light shade of reddish brown, and his smile seemed to warm the crowd.

"Ahhhh, Corey, Leila, *guten Abend!*" Hitler said as he saw them approach.

"Hey!" Corey said, pushing aside elbows. "Listen, we had a few things we wanted to talk to you about— *ow!*"

"You are still hurting, Corey!" Hitler said. "You are brave, strong. Like proper good German. *Bleib hier!* Stay here! You will enjoy *der schöne* Karl."

"'The handsome Karl'?" Leila said.

Hitler smiled. "This is what people call him. He is our mayor, Karl Lueger."

"*Mei-i-i-i-ne Damen und Herren!*" The man's voice boomed out over the square, without the help of a microphone. The crowd fell silent, and Lueger began to speak. He was slow at first, cracking a few German jokes that people laughed at. "Haw!!" Hitler guffawed. "He is very funny. He talks about the rats in our sewers, which are as big as *Pferde.* Horses. He gives them names. Schlomo. Chaim."

Jewish names.

Corey and Leila both stiffened. "Hilarious," Corey drawled.

As the man continued, his face grew somber, his eyes glowering. His words began taking a steady rhythm as his hands moved. He gestured to the crowd, pounding one fist into the other hand. His r's rolled and his p's spat.

Even though he didn't understand a word, Corey felt sweat trickling down the sides of his head. This guy's speaking style reminded him of Hitler in 1939. "What's he saying?" Corey whispered to Leila.

Her face was drawn and fearful. "Well, he made a transition from talking about rats to talking about Jews."

"But he's the *mayor*," Corey said. "There must be Jewish people living here. He has to represent them, right?"

"He's saying that they're sucking money from ordinary citizens," Leila said. "They're responsible for the poverty in the streets. They're dirty and . . . Do I need to go on?"

Corey shook his head.

Next to him, Hitler nodded. "*Ja*," he whispered. "Explains everything, no? So *klar*. Clear."

"*Wiener . . . über . . . Juden!*" Lueger bellowed.

Corey glanced at Leila. "'Viennese people over Jews,'" Leila translated.

"But that makes no sense," Corey said. "The Jewish people who live here *are* Viennese, right?"

"Wiener über Juden! Wiener über Juden! Wiener über Juden!"

Most of the crowd chanted in a bored, singsongy tone. But Hitler was shouting, his voice loud and screechy. His face was red and strained, his eyes almost not human. As if he'd transformed into some other creature.

Corey's blood froze in his veins. This was the man he'd seen in the Bürgerbräukeller. Not the hapless, homeless artist that people picked on in the streets.

Corey wasn't the only one to notice. Leila had grabbed on to his arm, her jaw hanging open in shock. She was seeing what he was. All around them, people cast startled looks toward Hitler. Some burst out laughing, others turned away. Even Mayor Lueger seemed a little thrown, his eyes darting toward the sound.

Right now, in 1908, the behavior may have been annoying and weird. But in a couple of decades, Corey knew, it would have a different effect. It would move three thousand people in a doomed restaurant to rise to their feet. And inspire an entire country toward a plan of mass murder.

23

"N—no," Corey said to Hitler. "No, I didn't think Handsome Karl was a good speaker. Or handsome."

It was hard to even look at him, let alone talk. Leila's face was pasty. She hadn't yet said a word.

Hitler was setting down his heavy shoulder bag across the street from the Café Central. Fritzie was long gone. After that display in town, so was Corey's appetite.

"All those things the mayor said about Jews . . ." Leila said. "It was wrong. People are people."

"Ach, Lueger does not mean this." Hitler's voice was raspy and hoarse from all the shouting. "He works with Jews in government. They are his friends. They love him very much. He loves them."

"That makes no sense," Leila said. "If they're his colleagues and friends, and they love each other, why does he want to kill them?"

Hitler looked surprised. "Kill? He does not say kill."

"But if he says he wants to get rid of them . . ."

Hitler waved a dismissive hand. "He is . . . how do you say . . . politic . . ."

"Politician," Corey said.

"There are many more who feel this way. Lueger speaks truth, but he is weak. The country is weak. This is because of the Jews, *Liebchen*. You will see this when you are older. They suck out all the marks—the money. Someday we will take it all back. Someday." Hitler reached into his sack and brought out two easels and stacks of paintings, drawings, and postcards. "I lost much time today, watching Lueger. So. You stay and help me sell?"

Corey gulped. His brain was racing. He could grab a rope, put it around this man's throat, and it would all be over.

If he were a murderer.

Think, he told himself. *Think this through.*

At this point in his life, even though Hitler was clearly a crackpot, he still thought he was talented enough to be an artist. But the dream was crumbling. He was shy and not very talented. He was poor, yet all around him he faced satisfied, well-fed people. He was a failure next to the geniuses who were already becoming famous. Every day brought more hits to his ego. He wasn't going to be able to take this forever. The more he failed, the more he'd need someone to blame. Someone besides himself.

Corey knew what was going to happen. Everyone in the future did. World War I was going to wreck Germany. The country would plunge into poverty. The Nazi party would form. Hitler would fail as an artist, and he would shift. He would give in to his anger. To that ugly, shrieking voice. The voice would gain power. It would convince others. That power would lead to death. Unless, right now, Corey and Leila did something radical.

Hitler had chickened out when he'd had the opportunity to apprentice with a genius. Somehow, they would have to make that happen.

Corey grabbed one of Hitler's paintings and held it lovingly in the sunlight. "Whoa. This is incredible. How much do you want for this one?"

Hitler shrugged. "Ach. *Vielleicht* five marks? It is not very good."

"Are you joking?" Corey said. "Only five? For *this?*"

He looked desperately at Leila. She nodded. "It's worth . . . seventeen," she said. "*Siebzehn.* At least."

"Haw!" Hitler's cheeks reddened as he smiled. "*Liebe Kinder!* You are young. I show to people. They say, two marks . . . three. Here is Vienna, not Stuttgart! Here is best artists in the world!"

"You need exposure," Corey said, but Hitler stared at him blankly. "It's not just about talent. You need for people to meet you. Important people."

"*Ja, ja, ja,*" Hitler replied, still neatly placing his work on the easels. "I know important people."

"Cool!" Corey said. "I mean, very good! Who?"

Hitler waggled his eyebrows, smiling at a woman dressed in furs who stared at his collection and then at him. She removed a cigarette from her mouth, blew smoke in his face, and left. "*Ach. Schreckliche Hündin!* She will see. Someday I go to meet these people. I will work for Herr Roller!"

"Alfred Roller? *The* Alfred Roller?" Leila said, shooting a quick glance to Corey. "You know him?"

"Not yet." Hitler tapped his pants pocket and raised an eyebrow. "I have letter of . . . how do you say . . . ?"

"Introduction!" Corey blurted out, quickly adding, "I'm guessing."

"His stage designs are *ganz dramatisch* . . . strong. Beautiful!" Hitler sighed. "But he is modern. Abstract. I am more . . . *klassisch*. Traditional. I am not certain he will like me. Or I will like him." He turned to pay attention to a hurried-looking man with wire-rim glasses, who was examining one of the paintings. "*Guten Abend!*" Hitler said. "*Dieses Kunstwerk kostet nur fünf Mark.*"

"*Fünf Mark? Ha! Schwindler* . . ." The man gave a derisive laugh and walked away.

"He calls me thief." Hitler's face darkened. "*Schwein.* He is thief! Banker. Steals from working people."

"I have an idea," Leila said. "My uncle Fritzie is playing piano tonight for a party at the opera house. Let's go—you, Corey, and me. Maybe Roller will be there."

Corey smiled. Leave it to Leila.

"Thank you," Hitler said. "But I will go to the house of Roller by myself . . . someday."

"Alone?" Leila said. "Just you and this world-famous guy? In his house? I wouldn't be brave enough to do that. I'd just freeze up! Think how much easier it is to meet people around a piano. Singing. Telling jokes. Maybe Fritzie can play your favorite song. You can sing! Herr Roller will be relaxed. He'll love you."

"*Ach,* I have bad voice . . . very bad." Hitler

nodded toward a young guy who was dressed in an expensive-looking black suit with a cape. *"Guten Abend! Möchten Sie ein Kunstwerk kaufen?"*

The man eyed Hitler's postcards carefully, looked at Hitler, and burst out hysterically laughing. *"Das ist keine Kunst!"*

"He asked the guy if he wanted to buy art," Leila whispered to Corey. "And the guy said, 'That is not art.'"

"Ouch," Corey said. "That's harsh. I don't know, sir. It's so tough to sell art on the street. You need to be in a place where people appreciate your talents."

As the man walked away, Hitler's shoulders sagged.

"Six o'clock?" Leila said. "In front of the opera house?"

"I will think about it," Hitler said with a sigh.

24

"What am I going to do with this?" Fritzie said, eyeing Hitler's landscape painting.

"It's nice, right?" Leila said. They were standing outside the Vienna Court Opera House. The sun was setting and the air had a chill. Fritzie was wearing a moth-eaten cloth coat and worn-out shoes.

"If you were Alfred Roller and you saw this," Corey said, "wouldn't you want to hire the artist?"

Fritzie glanced at it closely. "That man . . . he painted this? It is beautiful. In the old Viennese style but . . . lovely."

"His postcards suck," Corey said.

"*Entschuldig?*" Fritzie said.

"So, uh, here's the plan," Leila quickly interjected.

"When Hitler gets here, we're going to make sure he meets Roller. I'm thinking you musicians will be the star attraction. At some point you'll see Hitler. Treat him like he's a VIP. That will mean something. That will make everyone think he's something special."

"And we are doing this because—?" Fritzie said.

"Because your friend almost killed him," Corey said. "We owe him."

"This is his dream, to apprentice for Roller," Leila added. "So we'll make sure he and Roller meet. Then we'll show him this painting. Is there someplace backstage we can keep it?"

"We are not using the opera stage," Fritzie said. "But we have a room. A place where the performers gather before and after."

"Like a green room," Leila said.

"Can we bring Hitler and Roller there?" Corey asked.

Fritzie nodded. "It is tradition after the performance for honored guests to come to this room and greet performers. So yes. We will display this painting, if you like." He tucked the painting under his arm and began climbing the stairs. "Now we must go. I must not be late for Lotte. If I am late, she will tell me to perform in these clothes!"

"Um, you didn't bring any other clothes," Leila said.

Fritzie turned. "Ja. Lotte runs costume shop. They have formal clothing. All sizes. For the singers. Lotte knows musicians are poor. So she lends us very beautiful suits."

"All for one and one for all," Corey said.

"Come. They will let you in as my guests," Fritzie said. "If I am late for Lotte, I will blame you."

With a giggle, he flew up the stairs, painting in hand.

Hitler looked as out of place as a toad in an eagle's nest.

Leila cringed. Never in her life would she have dreamed she'd want to be Adolf Hitler's personal shopper. But his shirt collar was yellowing and lopsided, the designs on his tie looked suspiciously like food stains, and his shapeless pants were two inches short, exposing ripped white socks.

At the posh party in the rotunda of the Vienna Court Opera House, this would not do.

Leila eyed Roller. Fritzie had pointed him out when they'd walked in, a powerfully built man with a thick black beard and close-cropped hair. Fortunately, his back was turned. He was standing next to a gleaming, seven-foot grand piano. A crowd of adoring fans had gathered around him, looking up with eager smiles. But Roller's eyes were dark and impatient, darting restlessly toward a buffet table.

Hitler shuffled across the room, looking stooped and scared.

"Did you tell him it was a Halloween party?" Corey whispered to Leila. "Roller's going to roll with laughter."

Leila thought for a moment. "Remember what Fritzie looked like when he walked in?"

"He didn't look like that," Corey said.

"Yeah, but he was in casual clothes," Leila replied. "The woman who runs the costume shop, Lotte, was going to lend the musicians nice clothes. I say we bring Hitler back to the green room. Ask Fritzie to talk to Lotte. Maybe she'll take care of a poor artist."

Corey shrugged. "Worth a try, I guess."

Over Leila's shoulder, she heard a bellowing laugh from Alfred Roller. His circle of fans laughed with him. Leila knew she had to act fast before he turned completely around and saw Hitler's shabby-looking figure.

She waved in Hitler's direction. "Hey! Here we are!"

Hitler's face relaxed slightly at the sight of her and

Corey. He bounded toward them across the room, the cuffs of his pants flapping.

"I think I see fleas," Corey said.

"Be nice," Leila murmured. "Make him feel comfortable."

"Those sure are . . . shiny shoes!" Corey called out.

"Thank you," Hitler replied. "I'm afraid the rest is not so . . . beautiful? But it is best I can do. I borrow from my friend—"

"*Sssshhh*, no worries." Leila took him by the arm and walked him quickly toward the green room door. "Let's see if we can spruce you up."

Hitler sputtered in confusion, but Leila knocked on the door and asked to speak to Fritzie and Lotte. In a few moments Fritzie appeared, along with a stout, older woman who gasped at the sight of Adolf Hitler's outfit. Leila explained the situation to them. Fritzie listened with a kind, concerned smile. Then he turned to the older woman, who nodded curtly and whisked the poorly dressed guy inside.

"What did Fritzie say to her?" Corey asked.

"That he owed Hitler a favor," Leila replied. "My great-grandfather is a gem. He's taking this seriously. He feels guilty about what Otto did last night."

Ten minutes later, Hitler emerged wearing a clean

black suit that almost fit him. And a big, radiant smile. There wasn't much they could do about the hair, but he was standing up straighter. And Leila no longer felt like doubling over with laughter. "Very nice," she said. "And guess who is standing next to the piano? I hope you have your letter of introduction."

Hitler's eyes went wide with panic. Then he felt his pants pocket and exhaled. "Yes. I am ready."

As Fritzie stood by the piano, he was joined by a cellist, a violinist, and a clarinetist. They bowed, and everyone applauded in greeting. Leila brought Hitler right up close to Alfred Roller.

The crowd quieted as the group began playing a soft quartet. Hitler smiled. "Ahh, Brahms," he said, in Roller's direction.

"Brahms, *pah!*" Roller spat, with a foul sneer. "*Seine Musik ist bürgerlicher Müll.*"

"What does that mean?" Corey whispered.

"He doesn't like Brahms's music," Leila answered.

Hitler seemed to shrink. He stayed silent for the rest of the piece.

When it was over, the entire ballroom burst into applause. Roller, eyeing the buffet table, took the opportunity to get himself some food.

In German, Leila urged Hitler to follow. "I—I am not hungry," he replied.

"Go talk to Roller," Corey urged him. "There's no one else at the table. Be confident."

Hitler nodded and straightened himself out. With his shoulders flung back, he approached the buffet table. Leila moved closer, but she didn't want to be obvious. The next piece of music was beginning, and she could only catch snatches of conversation. The weather. The food. The tune.

Hitler's right hand seemed glued to the side of his pants. But soon it was slipping into his pocket, where he began pulling out a sheet of paper. "Yes . . . here we go," Leila murmured.

Now Hitler was holding out the letter of introduction and chattering away. Roller had speared a thick bratwurst and was chomping on it over a china plate. He glanced up as if Hitler were a hovering fruit fly. Finally, placing his plate down, Roller pulled a pair of glasses from his jacket pocket and took the note.

"He. Is. Reading it!" Leila squealed. She fought to stifle her voice, but she wanted to jump up and down.

"This is epic," Corey said.

"It's like . . . like taking the bullets out of John

Wilkes Booth's gun," Leila gushed. "Like locking up the nine-eleven hijackers at Logan Airport before boarding." She glanced back toward Fritzie and started to cry. "He has no idea what's happening right now. But he's going to be okay. This is amazing. He'll have a family, and they'll be okay too. Maybe we'll be listening to his recordings from Carnegie Hall."

"Uh . . . not so fast . . ." Corey said.

Leila spun back around. Roller was scowling. Asking Hitler pointed questions about his art experience. Hitler's face was red now, with sweat beading around his forehead. Whatever confidence he'd had was gone.

"Translate!" Corey whispered.

"He's yelling at Hitler. . . . How dare he bother him at a social event? . . . How can he judge a man's work if he can't see a sample? . . . Oh boy, this is not working."

Before she could finish, Corey was limping to the back of the hall as fast as his aching back could take him. He disappeared into the green room and emerged a few seconds later holding Hitler's painting. Leila intercepted him on the way to the buffet table. "What are you doing?" she demanded.

"Saving Hitler's butt." Swerving around Leila, he shouted, "Herr Roller, look!"

Hitler nearly jumped out of his shoes. He stared at

the painting as if it were about to explode.

Roller popped a cheese cube into his mouth and gave Corey an annoyed glance. As his eyes focused on the painting, Leila began to spin a story aloud to him. In German. Making it up as she went along.

She and Corey were students in the Vienna Academy of Fine Arts "youth department" . . . Herr Adolf Hitler was their teacher. . . . He was the finest artist they had met. . . . He dreamed of being a scenic designer. . . . He spoke about Alfred Roller as "a genius like the world had never seen."

She had never lied so much in her life.

Corey looked at her with his mouth hanging open. But Hitler began to nod. To smile and play along. "*Nein, nein . . .*" he murmured modestly. "*Liebe, süßes Mädchen.*"

(No, no. Dear, sweet girl.)

Alfred Roller peered over the top of his glasses frame, examining the painting carefully. "Hmm . . . mm-hmm . . ."

Leila stopped talking. She tried to read Roller's expression but couldn't.

Finally Roller grabbed a drink from the table and chugged some of it down. Giving Hitler a gruff look, he began speaking in German.

"What's he saying?" Corey whispered.

Leila listened carefully. "He's saying the work is old-fashioned . . . not at all Roller's style. But the sense of color is . . . admirable. It has a feeling of life . . . an emotional connection . . . and some other arty technical stuff I don't understand. Now he's asking if Hitler likes Gustav Klimt and Egon Schiele. . . ."

"Those are the really abstract artists?" Corey said.

"Right . . ." Leila replied. "So Hitler's, like, no, sorry, he's not a big fan, but he thinks that kind of style works . . . when it's onstage."

Corey smiled. "Whoa. Smooth. Maybe he's not as dumb as we think."

Roller stared at Hitler blankly for a long time. Then he let out what could have been a cough or a laugh, Leila wasn't sure. He glanced at the painting again, then handed it back to Corey. Heading back toward the piano, he grumbled over his shoulder to Hitler, *"Wir sehen uns am Montag pünktlich um acht Uhr in meinem Büro. Seien Sie bereit zu arbeiten."*

Hitler grabbed the edge of the table.

"What? *What?*" Corey said.

Leila could barely get the words out. "He said, 'I will see you in my office at eight sharp Monday morning. Be prepared to work.' And you, Corey Fletcher, are a genius. That's me talking."

"Aaaaaaaahh!" Corey screamed.

"Aaaaaaaahh!" Leila screamed.

They turned toward Hitler. But he was Hitler, so the idea of hugging him was off the table. "*Herzlichen Glückwunsch,*" Leila said. "Congratulations."

"I think," Corey said, "your future just changed."

"Yes." Hitler's eyes were full of tears. "And . . . I have you to thank. But . . ." His voice trailed off, as he glanced at the painting Corey had brought out.

"But what?" Leila said.

"That painting," he said. "I did not paint that."

Leila's mouth dropped open in surprise.

Corey thought of Fritzie's words the night before. *Otto knows this man by the bridge. Does not like him. He sells art on streets. Art painted by famous artists. For high money. But is not really the artist work.*

"It's bootleg?" Corey said.

Hitler looked at Leila. "*Was bedeutet 'bootleg'?*"

Leila shook her head and tried not to laugh. Behind her, Roller was calling to Hitler, gesturing toward his groupies, who were looking curiously at the new apprentice.

"Don't worry," Leila said. "Your secret is safe with us."

Corey smiled. No one would ever have to know.

Sometimes history was made with little lies.

As Hitler walked back toward Roller, he looked like he'd gained another inch in height. Corey still hated him.

That would never change.

"Did this really just happen?" Leila said softly.

"It did," Corey said, repeating it as if it would go away. "It did!"

"I . . . I don't . . . I can't . . ." Leila stammered.

"Let's go," Corey replied. "I don't want to spend another second in his sight."

As he reached into his pocket and grabbed onto some twenty-first century coins, Leila touched his shoulder.

25

Everything resets.

This was Corey's first thought as his eyes opened in Leila's room. When you change the past and come back, you're on a different timeline. Everything that has happened between then and now is affected. So when you return, there is no knowing what to expect.

Except the condition of Corey's back. Which was in utter, prickly-skin, pounding-head, teeth-grinding pain.

"Ohhhhhhh . . ." he moaned.

"We . . . we did it," Leila said. *"Corey, we did it!"*

Leila was still holding his shoulder. And Corey was still gripping the fistful of coins from the present, which had brought them back to where they started.

"Here," he said, thrusting the coins toward Leila. "My fortune for a healed back."

Leila let out a scream of excitement. "I don't believe this. Corey, do you realize what we just did? You are the most awesome human being who ever lived!"

She scooped him up in a hug, and he screamed.

"Oh! I'm so sorry!" Leila let go of him and spun to the window, throwing it open. "You need fresh air. We'll get you to a doctor. We'll do MRIs. X-rays. The best medications. A back transplant. Maybe back transplants are possible nowadays!"

"Back transplant?"

"Who knows? We changed time in a huge way, Corey! I'm going to call your papou and ask him to come over. He has to know about this. We need to tell him in person." She pulled out her phone and quickly called Corey's grandfather. "*Hi, Papou—I'm so glad you're there—it's Leila—we did it we did it please come over right away—we have so much to report—Corey is amazing!*"

"Right . . . right . . . amazing . . ." Corey was trying to let it sink in. But it didn't feel real yet. "Don't you think we ought to check what happened? You know, after Roller hired Hitler?"

"Of course! Of course! Oh. I have to calm down."

Leila shoved her phone in her pocket. She was practically dancing across the room. Her words were flying out at warp speed. "But one thing we know, Corey. Hitler never comes to power. Because of us, millions of people live! Scientists and doctors and shopkeepers and pop stars, and . . . and astronauts. Whatever. Who knows what things have happened. Maybe cancer is cured. Maybe New York City is now a suburb of Valley Stream—"

"What are you talking about?"

"I don't know! I'm just happy! Look! The good things didn't change. Central Park still exists, the air smells amazing, my family is still in the same apartment—"

Leila's door cracked open and her mom peeked in. "Is everything okay?"

"Mom! Mom! You're still Mom! Everything is *awesome!*" Leila said.

"Have you been bingeing on coffee ice cream again?" Mrs. Sharp asked.

"Mom! Mom! I have something I want to ask you. Some questions about history. Is that okay? It's for . . . a school project."

"Sure, sweetie," her mom said, sitting on the bed. "But I'm not great at history."

Did *anything* seem different? Corey wondered. Was her hair different? Her clothes? He wished he paid attention to things like that.

Leila shook the nervousness out of her hands. Corey could see her trying desperately to focus. To shovel out the adrenaline from her bloodstream. "Okay. Mom, did World War II happen?"

"Well, that's an easy one," she answered with a laugh. "Of course it did. Are these trick questions?"

"No." Leila swallowed hard. Corey sat next to her, putting his hand on her shoulder. "Mom . . . who were the Allies fighting in World War II? And what were the names of the leaders?"

"Japan," her mom said. "Under Emperor Hirohito . . . Wasn't that his name?"

"Yes," Leila said. "Yes, and . . . ?"

"Germany, of course. Under Hitler."

Wham.

Her words hung in the air like a bad stink. The war had begun in 1939. The Allies had joined it in 1941. Decades after Corey and Leila had left Vienna.

Corey could have tripled the pain in his back and it wouldn't have compared to how this felt.

"A-A-*Adolf* Hitler?" Corey said numbly.

"Of course," Ms. Sharp said.

"Tell me what he did, Mom," Leila went on. "Tell me about the Nazis. . . ."

Corey and Leila listened numbly as her mom began to list historical events.

It was all there.

Kristallnacht, the "shattering of glass," when the Nazis smashed down the shops run by Jews. That was there.

The roundups of Jews were there.

The camps.

The battles.

D-Day.

The Liberation.

How?

How could this have happened?

Leila kept asking questions—how many people died? How bad was it?—but after a while, Corey tuned it all out.

At some point the doorbell rang, but Corey barely noticed. He retreated to the corner and sat against the wall. The support made his back feel better. Leila's phone charger was on the windowsill within reach, so he plugged it into his dying phone.

Taking a deep breath, he did a quick search. Everything about the war, Nazis, and Hitler looked the same.

Which didn't make any sense. It couldn't be *exactly* the same.

Could it?

Finally he found an article about Hitler's youth that he recognized right away. He'd read this before. It had taught him about Hitler's three tries to meet Roller. It had described the failure. The burned letter.

With a creeping, dry-mouthed feeling, he read it carefully.

artist and stage designer, the famously loud and egotistical Alfred Roller. At the time Roller was the head designer of the Vienna Court Opera, one of the most prestigious positions in the cultural world. The letter was designed to gain Hitler an apprenticeship, in the hopes he would develop his skills and eventually become a successful artist. Hitler could not bring himself to meet Roller one-on-one, instead handing him the letter at a gala opera house party. Upon examining Hitler's work, Roller hired him immediately but fired him after three days, when he discovered that Hitler had forged the painting whose quality had secured him the job. In 1909 he applied to the Vienna Academy of Fine Arts. But now he was competing with future world-class artists, relying only on his own modest merits. He was rejected. Later in life Hitler claimed that this was the best thing to happen to him, as it pushed him into politics. In Vienna he was influenced by the rhetoric of the city's mayor, Karl Lueger,

It hadn't worked. The plan hadn't worked after all that.

He must have been staring at the text for a long, long time, because when he looked up, Leila was sitting with Papou. Her mom had left, and Leila was filling in the old man on the details. Corey hadn't even noticed his own grandfather entering.

"Hi, Papou," Corey said. "Did you hear what happened?"

"I did." The old man sat next to Corey and put his arm around his shoulders. He was wearing a soft cashmere sweater and it felt nice. "How are you, *paithaki mou?*"

"I'm going to go back," Corey said numbly.

"Mom's ordering brunch from the Mila Café," Leila said. "It'll be here soon."

"I didn't change the world, Papou," Corey said. "Nothing changed. Hitler lasted three days in his job, and then Roller fired him, and everything stayed the same."

"Wait, *what?* That's impossible!" Leila took the phone, still plugged in, and read the screen, too. Then she started tapping furiously, looking for more sources. "Holocaust . . . Alfred Roller . . . no . . . it can't be. . . ."

"We thought we'd de-Hitlered Hitler," Corey said.

"You set quite a task for yourself," Papou remarked.

Leila was crying now, but Corey was more angry than sad. "I could have done it, Papou. I had two good chances. I blew our chance to get him in Munich in nineteen thirty-nine, because I tried to protect someone named Maria who was helping us. In nineteen oh eight I saved Hitler's life by the river because I didn't know it was Hitler. Then I caused him to be fired from a job I helped him get, which would have changed his life and changed the world—"

"You didn't cause him to be fired, Corey!" Leila said.

"Yes, I did!" Corey insisted. "I butted in and gave Roller that dumb painting that really wasn't Hitler's work."

"But Hitler lied to you! He said it *was* his work! You didn't know!" Leila said. "Besides, Roller was about to blow him off when you stepped in. Without you, Hitler wouldn't have been hired at all."

"A lot of good that did," Corey said. "I'm a Throwback, Leila. I'm supposed to change things, remember? I have a superpower. And I even had you to help me. Why didn't I just bash him over the head myself while we had a chance?"

"Because you're a human being," Papou said. "You

did things you thought were right."

Corey stared out the window. Cars sped by on Central Park West, and someone was arguing about a parking space. Nothing was different. He knew he should have felt comforted by that, after the dangers of time travel. But all he felt was a knot in his stomach growing tighter and tighter.

"I'm going to go back to meet Hitler again," he murmured. "With a crowbar."

"And what if that doesn't work?" Leila said. "What if you get caught and die? This is hard to do, Corey. And you only have a limited number of tries anyway."

"It'll work," Corey murmured, trying not to feel numb inside. "I'll correct my mistakes, and it'll work."

"Corey, what you and Leila did was brave and dangerous and very smart," Papou said gently. Leila sat on the other side of the old man and rested her head on his shoulder. "Think about all you've done. Many, many things. You saved a soldier from suicide in the eighteen sixties. You saved Bailey from being run over. You stopped an evil man from mugging your sister. But you can't do it all."

"You guys don't know," Corey muttered. "You can't do what I can do. You're not Throwbacks."

"*Paithi mou*, maybe there are some things in history

that are just too big to change, even for Throwbacks," Papou said. "You can keep a stream from flowing, but you can't change the tides."

From outside the room, Corey heard the doorbell ring, followed by Ms. Sharp's footsteps running to answer the door.

"Come on," Leila said. "Food's here."

"*Etsi, bravo*," Papou said, rising to his feet on creaky knees. "*Ela*. Come to the kitchen. You will feel better."

As he left, Corey struggled to his feet. He unhooked his backpack and turned it upside down onto Leila's bed.

All that was left inside was a pair of Air Jordans and a metal cigarette case. The chandelier shard and the photo, the painting from Fritzie—they were gone now. Corey had left them in the past.

Even that he couldn't do right.

He pushed aside his sneakers. The cigarette case had fallen open to the beat-up old card inside that said "anislaw Meye." His mom's words came back to him.

Stanislaw Meyer . . . Mutti's brother. Your great-uncle. They found this on his body in the woods, near the end of the war.

He held the card and tried to remember the rest of his mother's story. An escape from a death march, through the woods. A road where Stanislaw was killed after he shot at Nazi vehicles that had actually been captured by Allies.

Killed because of a mistake.

Corey thought for a long moment. Even if he wanted to go back to 1908 Vienna, or the Bürgerbräukeller in 1939, he couldn't. The artifacts were gone now.

This cigarette case was found near the end of the war. Corey wasn't sure how near. By the time Stanislaw made his way through the woods, Hitler had probably done most of his dirty work.

But not all.

What if Stanislaw had not mistaken the convoy for Nazis? He would have survived. Mom had said he could see the lights of a town. If he could see them, he could have reached it. There, he might have had a chance.

Corey's mind was racing now. What about trying one more time?

A voice in his head screamed no. Papou had warned about this. *Once you start, it is so hard to stop. You get caught in what the ancients call a chaos loop. A cycle of failure and escalating frustration. It sucks you in and you will never, let go until . . .*

Chasing Hitler could become a chaos loop. Corey saw that now. What his grandfather had said about changing the tides made sense. Every superpower had a vulnerability.

"Corey *mou!*" Papou called out from the kitchen. "Come before the bagels get stale!"

Corey heard the words but didn't move.

He knew he couldn't just give up. Saving a man's life—*that* wasn't trying to change the tides. That was something he had done before, and he could do it again.

Corey took a deep breath. "Forgive me, Papou," he said softly. "Forgive me, Leila."

"Eh?" Papou called back. "Did you say something? Corey, come! Ach, what is with my grandson?"

Papou's footsteps padded down the hallway toward Leila's room. But Corey was already gripping tight to the cigarette case.

He heard a hand on the doorknob. He saw it turn.

As the door angled open, he was gone.

26

The cold was a deep shock to his system.

So was the sight of the corpse.

It—he—was facedown in the snow. The dead man was dressed in a thick but ragged wool coat. A deep oval of blood was growing in the snow from the top of his head outward.

Corey felt sick to his stomach. He had to look away.

Instinctively he backed off. But the ground rose sharply behind him and he stumbled. The snow was seeping through his shoes, and already his feet were freezing. Above him the sun shone through the gray-green peaks of a pine forest. Corey could see a shack at the top of the incline. The corpse had been left by the side of a path recently beaten through the snow. The footsteps were fresh, their outlines only now being softened by thick, falling flakes. They traced the bottom of the hill and disappeared into the woods.

In the distance he heard tromping feet and voices— shouts and commands in some other language. It sounded like German to Corey, but he couldn't be sure. The metal cigarette case belonged to Uncle Stanislaw, and he was Polish.

In the area where the voices were coming from, Corey could see movement. A dull gray blot among the trees, popping in and out of sight.

As he stood, his back ached again. He kept himself from crying out in pain. He couldn't risk being heard in the clear wintry air and the empty forest. Someone in the group obviously had a gun. And was not afraid to use it.

Corey's teeth began to chatter. He knew he wouldn't last long standing here in just a shirt and pants.

He stole another look at the corpse. The coat looked raggedy, but it was made of wool. The boots were a little big, and they had holes, but they were thicker and sturdier than what Corey was wearing. And the dead man's hands were covered with shredded leather gloves.

Corey choked back a feeling of nausea. The idea of

taking clothing from a dead person was disgusting.

But not disgusting enough to die for.

Kneeling down, he took a deep breath and said softly, "I'm really sorry, sir. If you're listening to me from wherever you are, forgive me, okay?"

He waited a moment, then reached for the jacket collar. The man was rail thin, but he still seemed heavy. Pulling downward, to avoid the growing bloodstain, Corey carefully removed the coat. The body was still warm, and somehow that fact made Corey finally give up whatever was in his stomach. It wasn't much, but it steamed when it hit the snow.

He coughed and coughed. Loud, retching coughs. He tried to stifle the sound but couldn't. The voices in the distance were growing louder, but it sounded like the men were arguing. No one seemed to have heard him.

The coat was heavy and about two sizes too big, but putting it on, Corey felt warmer right away. As fast as he could, he removed the guy's boots and put them on, too. And then the gloves. "Thank you," he whispered.

Lifting his feet awkwardly with the oversized boots, he headed up the hill toward the shack. The snow was fluffy but very thick, which made the going slow. The shack was lopsided and neglected. Its only door had been torn off, and if there had ever been windows or screens, they were long gone. The rusted black pipe of a stove emerged upward through a small, slanted roof, which looked like it was about to slide off its beams.

It was shadowy inside as Corey leaned into the door. "Hello?" he called out.

No answer.

As he stepped in, the ground was soft and bouncy under his boots, fragrant with decaying branches and pine needles. He propped his back against a wall and allowed himself to sink down. In the cold, his pain wasn't quite so horrible. He could still hear the voices down on the path. It seemed like the men were standing still, maybe taking a break. German. Definitely German. Soon they gave way to laughter, light talking. And then, finally, silence.

Leila would know what they were saying.

Of course.

Corey felt himself seize up inside. He was more scared than he'd been in a long time. What made him think he could do this without Leila? Making decisions when you were tired and depressed was a dumb idea. Where was he anyway? What year was this? He knew nothing.

He would have to go back. He would have to convince Leila to do this with him.

Corey felt a funny sensation on his legs. He looked down in time to see a small rat leaping off his pants and onto the floor.

"Gahhhh!" he cried out.

The rat twitched its whiskers and scurried into a hole.

Enough.

He took off his gloves and reached into his pocket for his twenty-first-century coins. Those would get him back to the present. Right away he noticed the cigarette case was gone. He must dropped it down by the corpse.

He looked around for something else, some other piece of metal in the shack that would eventually get him back here, with Leila. But the place was in such a state of decay. It looked like it had been put together with glue anyway. He took a deep breath. Before doing anything else, he would have to go back down the hill and get the case. He stood and moved for the door.

A sharp bang, from deep in the woods, made him jump.

Then another bang.

A scream rang out over the snow, followed by a series of explosions like firecrackers. Screams. Blood-curdling howls.

Corey couldn't move. It felt as if every organ had shriveled, every ounce of fluid in his body drained. He stood still in the silence that followed, which was absolute. As if nothing at all had happened.

He felt like puking again. Puking and going home.

He would do this fast. Grab the cigarette case, then grab the coins in his pocket. His twenty-first-century coins. *Did he even have coins anymore, in these clothes from 1939?* Corey wasn't even sure of that. He'd used them to get back to the present, but had he even put them back in his pocket when he'd changed into these clothes at that store in Munich?

As he fumbled in his pocket, his hands were so cold he couldn't feel his fingers. Even with the gloves. They closed around something, but he wasn't sure what. The dumbest thing he'd done was not wear a belt with a metal buckle, from home. As a backup.

He tried to pull his hand out, but it caught on the edges of his pocket. Which would have been funny if it wasn't so pathetic. With a grunt, he pulled it loose.

His fist was full of coins, all right. But they spilled

out onto the ground, scattering on the forest floor like tiny animals. Some of them disappeared into the shadows, but three coins rolled right out the door.

Corey ran after them, but he didn't get very far.

A massive figure stepped into the doorway, blocking his way.

27

"Sssshhhhhh . . ."

Corey didn't need the warning. He was too scared to make a noise. He retreated into the shack until his back made contact with the wall.

The man stood there, staring. His face was broad and pockmarked and covered with sweat. His eyes were dark, but strands of reddish hair flowed out the sides of a thick wool cap, almost to his shoulders. He wore a coat not much different from the one Corey had taken from the dead body, and he looked as shocked as Corey felt. "*Junge* . . ." he said under his breath.

Corey recognized that German word. "Boy!" he said. "Yup. I'm a boy. A helpless one. So don't kill me."

"*Englisch?*" the guy asked.

"American."

Taking a deep breath, the guy walked in. "You dropped coins. But I do not think you will need them here. The wolves, they do not accept cash."

"Wolves?" Corey said

"I am not afraid of many things." The guy chuckled. "But I am very much afraid of wolves. It is why I do not like *der dunkle Wald.*"

"I don't speak German."

"The dark forest."

The guy had to duck to fit through the door. His shoulders were enormous. He seemed to take up most of the space in the room. Not to mention the air. Corey was finding it hard to breathe.

He stared at Corey, scratching his head. "Why are you here?"

"Why are *you* here?" Corey asked.

"To make peepee." He gestured toward one side of the shack. Then he gave the tiniest hint of a smile. "But I am finished."

The man went right for the window. He grimaced as he lowered himself to one knee and peered through, in the direction of the shots. For a moment he stared, not moving a muscle. "I hear nothing," he said finally.

"No," Corey agreed.

"Do you have gun?" he asked, his eyes not wavering. "Knife?"

"Sorry."

"The shots. Outside. You heard them, yes?"

"Yes."

Bullets. Wolves.

Get me out of here.

"I . . . sort of have to go," Corey said lamely. He eyed the holes in the snow, just outside the door, which marked where the coins had dropped.

"No!" The man grabbed Corey's arm and pulled him down onto his knees. "It is not safe."

"Right. Okay, I'll stay a few minutes."

"They tell us—all of us—we are the best workers in camp. . . ." The man's voice was raspy and strained. His eyes darted as he spoke, and his words spilled out over one another. "They say they are taking us to freedom. To border town near Austria called Kurtstadt. We have food, drink while we are walking. Then one man, Oskar, he is very sick. He asks them to *warten*. Wait. But it is so cold, and they are not patient. They tell him come, come, *schnell*, we must go! Oskar tries, but he cannot move. And so they shoot him. *In den Kopf*. In the head. Just like that. They say this is act of kindness.

236

Because otherwise he will die slowly in snow. Kindness!"

The man's eyes were red and moist now.

Corey gulped. "I think I'm wearing Oskar's coat."

But the man didn't seem to hear him. He was talking as if to the air. "They say they will take the rest of us to freedom. But we must walk. This is when I know they are not telling the truth. They do not want to walk. They do not want to go all the way to another Nazi camp in the cold. They want to return. And if they return with no prisoners, pffft, the Nazis do not ask questions. They do not care what happened to us. So I tell guards then I must go and peepee, and I hope they do not notice I am gone. . . ."

"Yeah. I hope so, too."

The man whirled around to Corey. "Who are you?"

"My name is Corey Fletcher," he replied.

"Because when I come up the hill, I find this in the snow." He held out the metal cigarette case to Corey. "Yours?"

"Uh, yes. Thanks." Corey reached for the box, but the man pulled it back.

"Not so fast," he said. "One question."

"What?"

The man eyed him oddly. "If your name is Corey, then why you have a cigarette case with this card on the inside?"

He flipped open the box and lifted out the ID card, which was now newer looking and intact, displaying the name STANISLAW MEYER.

Corey thought fast. "Because that's my . . . uncle. My Polish uncle. He gave this to me. I'm using it as an alias. Because the Nazis are after my family. I was sent away. I don't want anyone to know my real name."

"Ah." The guy snapped the box shut and handed it to Corey, who quickly stashed it in his pocket. "This is a coincidence. Because this name, Stanislaw Meyer— this is my name, too. And I have a case that is exactly same."

28

By now Corey had watched Leila come face-to-face with her ancestors twice. So he should have known how to handle this meeting. Running into these ancestors made sense. That's what the artifacts did—they brought you to the people who owned them.

But all that came out of his mouth was incoherent splutter. "You—you're Stan—wow—I mean—the same name—"

The big guy reached into his pocket, pulled out the identical cigarette case, and flipped it open. Inside were a few battered-looking cigarettes, some of which had already been smoked down to nubs. With his yellowing fingertips poking through his gloves, he pushed aside the cigarettes and pulled out his ID card. The identical Star of David. The identical name.

He didn't look at all like Mom. That was the first thing Corey noticed. But his face was dirty and he was dressed in heavy clothing, so it was hard to tell. As he looked at Corey, his gaze was steely and direct. And his smile curled up on the left side. Those were definitely family traits.

"If your name is Fincher," he said, "it is maybe not wise to take an alias as a Jewish name."

"It's Fletcher," Corey said. "My family is Jewish on my mother's side."

At least that was true.

"Mm," Stanislaw said, pocketing his case. "We are maybe related."

"Maybe," Corey said.

Crouching to his knees, Stanislaw looked back out the window. "We cannot stay here long."

"Where do we go?" Corey asked.

"Sssshhh . . ." Stanislaw put his finger to his mouth, gesturing outside with his eyes.

Corey knelt next to him. The snow had picked up, so it was hard to see very far. Overhead the wind rustled in the pine trees, howling piteously like a lost ghost.

"Ach," Stanislaw whispered. "We stay here too long already. Look to the right."

As his eyes adjusted to the brightness, Corey saw a vague shadow in the whiteness. It began to grow, until he could make out individual shapes. Two . . . three . . . four . . .

"Five guards?" Corey asked.

Stanislaw nodded. "And we were thirty prisoners. We outnumber them six to one. But they have guns. And power. And no souls."

"Our footprints!" Corey said. "They'll lead here!"

"No," Stanislaw said. "Look. Do you see our prints now? Nature takes care of us."

He had a point. The forest floor was a field of blowing snow. Whatever prints had been there were now covered over.

They both ducked down under the windows as the men came into view. Although their prints had been covered, too, Corey could see that their path had been carefully marked. They had driven metal tags, in the shapes of swastikas, into tree trunks using nails.

Soon they were passing directly underneath, talking steadily. "What are they saying?" Corey asked.

As Stanislaw listened, the lines on his face seemed to deepen. "We killed them all. That's what he is saying. Killed every one of them. Shot them in a barn. Where they . . ." The words choked in his throat and he cleared it. "Where they belonged."

That was good for a big belly laugh among the guards, and another flurry of words. Stanislaw listened again and translated for Corey: "This one who speaks now, he is angry that he gave some schnapps—schnapps, that is a drink—to one of the prisoners. Because now there is none left. And the next guard . . . he is saying, he should go back and squeeze it out of the prisoner."

That drew the biggest laugh of all.

"That's disgusting," Corey said.

"Yes." Stanislaw's face was deep red. The veins in his neck stood out like ropes. Now Corey could hear the soft thump of footsteps coming nearer. He began to raise his head but Stanislaw pushed him down. "*Nein!*" he said, in a voice barely a whisper. "This man is coming here . . . he said he needs to pee."

Stanislaw's teeth were clenched tight now. His eyes stared at the wall so hard that he could almost imagine them burning a hole through it. "I want him to suffer here," he murmured. "He must know what it feels like."

"Wait," Corey whispered. "You wouldn't try to do anything, right? They'll hear you!"

"*Ja, ja.*"

Corey tried to stay as small and quiet as he could. His breaths and Stanislaw's rose in little white puffs. They both tried to bury their mouths in their sleeves. The man was singing now, way out of tune, getting louder and louder.

Corey stopped breathing. He eyed his dropped coins again, just outside the door. The guard was on the opposite side of the house. Directly beyond the wall now. Maybe six inches away. If Corey were to move across the room or sneeze, or if the guy decided to poke his head in through the window, he and Stanislaw would be dead meat.

The singing became a hum. And then, a shout from below: "*Schwein! Mach schnell! Wir gehen! Es ist spät!*"

"*Ja, ja, ja* . . ." the man replied, so close Corey felt his voice vibrating the wall.

The voices continued, growing fainter. Stanislaw made walking motions with his fingers and silently mouthed the words, *They are going.*

Corey heard the dull clinking of an unclasped belt buckle. The man's hum became a whistle. Stanislaw drew himself into a crouch. He crab walked around Corey until he was under the window. Outside, the guard was relieving himself and enjoying the sound of his own shrill whistling. Stanislaw crouched, his eyes trained upward.

What was he doing? Corey tried to catch his glance. He shook his head as hard as he could. But as the guards' voices dimmed, Stanislaw's expression seemed to grow firmer.

Finally, like a gymnast, Stanislaw sprang upward and out the window. Twisting to the left, he wrapped his arms around the guard in a wrestling hold.

"*Was ist . . . Hallo! . . cccchh . . .*" The man was choking, trying to get out of Stanislaw's grip. Stanislaw planted himself and leaned back hard, lifting the guard off his feet and into the window opening. The guard tried to spread his legs to jam himself in the frame, but the old wood just splintered. The two men came crashing through, tumbling onto the floor.

With a superquick move, Stanislaw grabbed the pistol from the guard's belt. Holding it in two hands, he stood and pointed it at the man's head.

The guard stayed flat on his back, staring up at Stanislaw and Corey, his face ashen with fear and bewilderment. "*Sie . . .*" he said to Stanislaw.

Corey knew that word. *You.*

"Ah, he recognizes me," Stanislaw said. "For the

first time, he sees me as a human. What is my name? *Wie heiße ich?*"

The guard's eyes went wide. "*Ich . . . ich weiss nicht.*"

"He doesn't know. Of course." Stanislaw cocked the gun. "Say my name. *Sagen Sie meinen Name!*"

The guard flinched. "*Das kann ich nicht!*"

"You—you're not going to shoot him . . ." Corey said.

"The other guards walked off without him," Stanislaw said. "As I said, they are not patient fellows. Even for each other."

"They'll hear the shot," Corey said. "They'll come back for him."

"Perhaps," Stanislaw replied. "Though it sounds like they have hurried away. Perhaps this is their joke, eh? They are so funny."

He spat out that last word, jettisoning saliva into the guard's face.

"Let's just go!" Corey said.

But Stanislaw wasn't budging. "I know his name," he said, leaning down until the gun was inches from the man's eyes. "Heinrich. He is one of the worst. He is the man who killed Oskar. He did it while yawning. To make the others laugh. This he likes to do very much. And now, listen—they laugh at you!"

Heinrich began to cry, pleading.

"What a surprise," Stanislaw said. "You *do* have blood in your veins, yes? I wasn't sure. I thought it was ice. Maybe now we shall spill it, for the men you slaughtered."

As he translated that into German, Heinrich let out a squeal. *"Nein . . . bitte! Die andere werden kommen."*

"The others will come, he says," Stanislaw said. *"Vielleicht nicht. Vielleicht sind Sie in ihren Augen nur ein Tier."* Perhaps not. Perhaps to them, you are no more than an animal. But I do not believe you are an animal, Heinrich. I believe you are a man. And so I will treat you like one. My name is Stanislaw. And I will give you something you do not deserve. It is called mercy."

Rearing back with his right hand, he whacked Heinrich in the head with the butt of the gun. Hard.

With a grunt, the guard fell still.

Stanislaw shoved the pistol into his pocket. "We go," he said. "We must be very far away when the pigs return."

29

Corey followed Stanislaw out the door. He was climbing up the hill when he remembered his coins. Quickly he ran back and looked for them by kicking up the snow. One . . . two . . . three.

Perfect. That would be enough. He stooped to pick them up and shoved them back into his pocket. He would need them.

"Wait for me!" Corey cried out.

He caught up to Stanislaw at the top of the hill, where the forest thickened and they could easily hide if they needed to. The wind had picked up, whipping the snow from below their feet. The sunlight was dimming behind the clouds.

Stanislaw beat a twisted path through the trees. But

it wasn't until they'd been walking for a half hour that Corey saw he was limping.

"Are you all right?" he asked.

Stanislaw stopped, breathing hard. He gazed tensely back in the direction of the shack. But they were way too deep into the trees to be noticed. "Yes, I am all right," Stanislaw said. "Back in the camp, before we marched, they beat me. Because I gave my bread to a child."

"They *beat* you for that?"

He took off his cap. Under it was a dirty, blood-soaked bandage. The wound was just above Stanislaw's left ear, and the blood was outlined in a yellowish white.

Corey winced. "That's getting infected."

"Yes." Slowly Stanislaw put his cap back on. "The Nazis are crazy. They know they are losing the war, and this makes them crazier. I know this. They are moving prisoners from place to place. To hide us. To hide their shame."

"This will sound like a dumb question," Corey said, "but can you tell me today's date?"

Stanislaw thought for a moment. "February nineteen forty-five. Maybe fifth? Sixth? I do not know exactly."

Corey nodded. Nineteen forty-five was the year the war ended. "This is going to work out. It will be over soon."

"Yes, I believe so," Stanislaw replied. "Sometimes I hear them talk. They are afraid. When we go to villages, I hear radio also. The Allies have learned about the camps. So the Nazis, they need to do something. The weak prisoners, they kill. But those of us who are strong, who can work, they march us from camp to camp. Already I have been to many. Theresienstadt, Auschwitz, Sachenhausen, Flossenbürg, Ganacker. Sometimes we go in trains, sometimes we march on foot. Each camp is worse than the other. I see my family shot, hanged. Why do I live? Because I am lucky. Nothing more. Yesterday we are in Traunstein, Germany. We stop at a farm. This is where I meet a Resistance spy. I can tell by the eyes. I can always tell. Her name is Marlene. No one suspects. She milks the cows! She gives me a map, and I go to toilet to read it. But I stay a long time. Heinrich notices this. He comes into toilet to find me. And for this—for this I am beaten for second time."

Stanislaw led Corey to a tree stump. He sat, quickly rolling up his right pant leg and rolling down his sock.

"The fool," Stanislaw said with a snort, pulling out a sheet of paper from inside his sock. "He did not see the map. I hid it."

But Corey was staring at a sharp bulge above Stanislaw's ankle. The skin around it was bright red. "That's where the guy beat you?"

"With a metal pipe," Stanislaw said. "He aimed higher. But I fell."

Corey cringed. "It looks broken. I don't know how you can put weight on it. Even looking at it hurts. How did you manage to pull that guard through the window?"

Stanislaw let out a low whistle. He covered his leg up again and stood. "It feels much better if I don't see it."

Corey knew he'd been given some kind of superpower. But for strength or bravery, nothing he'd done compared to his great-uncle Stanislaw.

They huddled over the map, trying to shield it from the wind and snow. It was hand drawn with teeny writing, in crazy detail. A path, drawn in deep red, led through the woods. Each turn was indicated with a landmark—a tree with an almost human shape, the ruins of a hut, a steep valley. The last part of the journey was along a river. The path ended at a big star, just beyond the forest. Over the star was the word KURTSTADT.

"I believe," Stanislaw said with a smile, "we are on the right track. You see that, where I am looking? It is the first turn marked on the map."

He pointed straight ahead. Looming over the forest was a tree that looked like it had been growing since the dinosaur days. Like some kind of gnarled, petrified, mutant tyrannosaur.

"From there, we go left," Stanislaw went on. "And we follow. It is important to memorize this path."

He ran his fingers along the paper from landmark to landmark. Corey concentrated hard, trying to commit it all to memory. Stanislaw pointed to the village at the end of the path, marked Kurtstadt.

"Here," Stanislaw said, "is where Heinrich and the Nazi pigs were taking us. I was so happy. You see, in Kurtstadt the Resistance has set up a trap."

"What are they trapping?"

"Not what. *Who.*" Stanislaw gave Corey a full smile for the first time. The sight of that smile hit Corey hard. It was his mom's face in his great-uncle. "Kurtstadt is very . . . far from other places."

"Isolated," Corey said.

"Ja. Not many people know it is there. One of the Nazi officers, he was born there. So the Nazis believe this is a good place to hide from the Allies. They plan to gather in Kurtstadt and then make disguises." Stanislaw shrugged. "In a short time, they plan to leave. They make their way across Europe to Atlantic ports. From there they board ships to South America. They feel they must do this or the Allies will capture them. In Brazil, in Argentina, they will get lost."

"Can't someone stop them?" Corey asked. "I mean, if *you* know about it—"

"Yes, *mein Junge.*" Stanislaw nodded. "I know something else, too. Something the Nazis do not know. You see, the Resistance has captured Kurtstadt. They set up shops, move in families, make a school—every person in the village is a Resistance member. Ha! This week, maybe next, Himmler and Göring arrive. Marlene believes Hitler will be with them, but she is not sure."

Himmler. Göring.

Corey could still see their smug faces marching down the center aisle of the Bürgerbräukeller. And walking like a triumphant king, his failed art career long behind him, Adolf Hitler.

But that was 1939, and now it was already 1945. It was too late to save most of the lives Hitler destroyed. And way too late to turn him into a famous stage designer. But the war would still be going on for a few more months. The Nazis would be accelerating their murders in desperation. And Hitler would stay in power until he committed suicide. Because history showed that he did this. Which meant the plan at Kurtstadt was destined not to work.

And Stanislaw was destined to die there. Because of a mistake.

But destiny could be changed. Until now, Kurtstadt had never had a Throwback. And mistakes could be reversed.

"I'm on board with this," Corey said. "I am so on board."

Stanislaw let out a triumphant laugh, carefully folding the map and putting it in his pants pocket. As he stepped forward, he nearly fell. Corey grabbed his arm, but Stanislaw brushed him off. "I will be fine," he said. "Being in Kurtstadt to see Herr Hitler's face—this gives me strength."

The big guy was moving a lot slower, so Corey stayed close. Stanislaw's wool cap was changing color now, too. The blood from his first beating was seeping through, and his face was growing paler.

The next landmark was a battered, roofless old hut, not unlike the one where they had met. By the time they got there, the clouds had lifted. It was no longer snowing, and the air felt crisp. Overhead the sun was beginning to set. The decayed remains of a carriage lay covered in snow outside the hut. The interior floor looked no different than the floor of the rest of the forest. "It . . . gets dark . . . in the woods . . . early," Stanislaw said. "Maybe . . . we rest. Ankle . . . hurts."

He was struggling to speak now. His right hand darted up to touch his head, near the injury. Corey couldn't be sure, but it looked like his head was swelling. The ankle injury could probably wait the night, but not the head.

"The hut doesn't give us any shelter or warmth," Corey said. "We're halfway there. If there are doctors in Kurtstadt, we should keep going."

"We will not have enough light," Stanislaw remarked.

Corey could see the faint outline of a full moon against the dark blue sky, through the branches of the pines. That was a good thing, for starters. He quickly fished out his phone and saw it was about 70 percent charged. Turning it toward his great-uncle, he toggled the flashlight on and off.

"Aaaagh!" Stanislaw screamed. *"Was ist das?"*

Corey grinned. "Make it to Kurtstadt, get healthy, and I'll tell you where to invest your money in a few decades."

30

Stanislaw wouldn't die in the middle of a forest, Corey told himself. He knew this from his mom's story. Dying in the forest was not Stanislaw's destiny.

But Corey also knew that he'd entered his great-uncle's life as a destiny-changer. With time travel, all bets were off. Stanislaw could barely move his legs now, and he wasn't making much sense. At least when he was remembering to speak English.

"Come on, Stan," Corey said, his arm wrapped around his great-uncle's shoulders. "You can do this. The valley is our last landmark before the river. And you know what comes after the river, right?"

"*Ja*," Stanislaw said. "Wiener schnitzel."

"No, Kurtstadt!" Corey said. "Remember Kurt-stadt?"

"Ah!" Stanislaw shook his head and blinked a few times. "So sorry. I was dreaming . . . about dinner. Isn't that funny, dreaming while standing up?"

Descending into the valley had been easy. And the floor of the valley was mostly meadow, which meant they could head straight across it.

They slogged through that slowly. "Can you make it up?" Corey asked. He held tight to Stanislaw's arm as the ground began to rise.

Stanislaw didn't answer. With each step he seemed to get heavier. He stopped every few seconds. He didn't seem to be losing any more blood from his wound. But the infection had been festering a few more hours, and it looked awful.

About halfway up, Corey felt Stanislaw's legs buckle. His weight nearly took Corey down with him. "I . . . am afraid . . . you should . . . leave me here," Stanislaw rasped.

"Nope," Corey replied. "Out of the question."

"I command you!" Stanislaw peeled Corey's hand off his shoulder. "Go. I stay here. I rest. You will find a doctor and come back to me."

Instead of obeying, Corey took his great-uncle's arm and draped it over his shoulders. The guy was at least eighty pounds heavier, and a lot stronger, but Corey was easily as tall. In Stanislaw's weakened state, Corey had some leverage. "I'm not letting go," Corey said, "if I have to carry you."

"Ha!" Stanislaw blurted out. "You are . . . *ein ungewöhnlicher Junge.*"

"You don't have to insult me," Corey said.

"It means, 'an unusual boy,'" Stanislaw said. "It is meaning to be a good thing. You are kind. And brave."

Corey smiled. "That's what family is all about."

He cringed as the words left his mouth. The last thing he needed to do was explain what *that* statement meant.

But Stanislaw showed no reaction.

Together they trudged uphill, the weight on Corey's shoulders getting heavier with each step. Not twenty feet before the top, Stanislaw buckled again. And this time, when he fell, Corey went with him.

They both rolled downhill. Corey flailed, trying to grab something. Anything. With each inch they were giving back ground they'd worked so hard to gain.

Finally Stanislaw's body slammed against a sturdy

holly bush and stopped. Corey reached out. His hand closed around the big guy's bad ankle and Stanislaw let out a strangled cry.

"Sorry!" Corey let go and scrambled to his feet.

"I want . . . to die."

"No!" Corey shouted. "That is out of the question!" His voice echoed up the sides of the valley. His heart was racing. Taking his phone from his pocket, he turned on the flashlight and shone it up the slope.

Forty feet. Maybe fifty. That was all the distance they'd sacrificed in the fall.

"We can do this," Corey said. He pocketed his phone and dug both his arms under Stanislaw's. Planting his feet as firmly as he could, he pulled up. "Heeeeeave . . . ho!"

There was never a moment in his life when he wished he could trade in time-hopping for aging. But he did now. Because the twenty-five-year-old Corey, he knew, could lift this dead weight a whole lot better.

Stanislaw was not budging. His eyes were shut. He was muttering something in German.

"How did you do this?" Corey murmured under his breath. "In actual history, you got through the forest on your own. Without me. *How?*"

Corey tried to remember the details from his mother's story about Stanislaw. He had gone to pee. He had escaped being shot. He had made the long walk—this long walk—until he reached a road to civilization. And just before getting there he'd found a dead soldier and taken his gun.

Emerging onto the road, he saw a convoy of Nazi vehicles approaching. He could see they saw him. So in panic, he shot at them. They shot back. . . . The convoy was captured vehicles. . . . Resistance fighters soldiers were driving them.

Taking a deep breath, Corey braced himself. He had to be prepared. If he was able to keep Stanislaw from dying of exposure, right here, he'd still have to watch out for the convoy. For the death his great-uncle was destined to have. He could not let Stanislaw be killed like that, at the hands of Resistance fighters because of a mistaken identity.

"One more time, Stan," Corey said, squatting behind his great-uncle and pulling upward. "U-u-u-u-u-up!"

This time, Stanislaw jerked himself to his feet. "Gaaaah!" he gasped.

Corey fell back with the momentum, landing on his rear. He followed Stanislaw's glance to the edge of a wooded glade not thirty yards away. A silver-gray wolf was loping toward them with slow, graceful steps. Its head was heavy and low to the ground, its fur thick and mottled.

It stared at them, its eyes yellow-green in the reflected moonlight, growling softly. And then it sat on its haunches and threw its snout straight up, revealing a thick white neck. Its howl echoed, high and fierce.

"D-d-d-does it attack humans?" Corey asked.

"I don't know! Maybe it's trying to tell us something. But I do not want to find out! I am very much afraid of wolves. And this one is a monster!" Stanislaw reached into his own jacket, but his hands were flailing. "The gun. Use Heinrich's gun!"

As the wolf loped closer, Corey dug his hand into Stanislaw's jacket and pulled the gun out from the inner pocket. It was about five times heavier than he expected, and it dropped into the snow.

"Hurry!" Stanislaw said.

"I don't know how to use it!" Corey said, scooping up the weapon.

"*Just shoot it!*"

Now the wolf was picking up speed. Corey lifted the gun. He pointed it toward the wolf but the barrel wobbled. Now he could hear the wolf chuffing, sending puffs of breath. The sight of the gun didn't seem to frighten it one bit.

"Aaaaghhhhh!" Stanislaw yelled.

"Aaaaghhhhh!" Corey echoed.

He lifted the gun to the sky and squeezed the trigger as hard as he could.

CRRRRRACK!

The shot rang out, and Corey recoiled backward. As he fell into the snow, he took Stanislaw with him. Lying down, they might as well have been flashing a sign saying EAT DINNER HERE, WOLVES WELCOME!

Corey scrabbled to his feet and braced himself. He fumbled with the gun again, sure the wolf was in mid-leap.

But the creature was sitting on its rear. Staring. Startled by the noise and assessing its next move. It was so close Corey could swear he smelled dead meat on its breath.

"*Gehen wir*," Stanislaw said, grabbing the gun from Corey. "We go. Now!"

Corey pulled Stanislaw to his feet and tried to hook his arm around his shoulders again.

This time, his great-uncle didn't need the help. For a badly injured man, he was moving up the slope just fine.

* * *

The wolf was far behind them when they reached the river. Stanislaw's burst of energy had sapped him in more ways than one. As they slogged along the banks, he could not stop talking. "We will vanquish all of them," he said, his voice slurred. "Goebbels, Hitler, Himmler, Rommel, Hanftstängl, Gitler, Hommel, Pretzel . . ."

At some point, Corey thought, he was just making up names. His head looked about two sizes too big. He prayed that the doctors in Kurtstadt would be able to treat this infection before it was too late.

In the middle of his list of names, Stanislaw let out a scream. "What?" Corey asked. "What happened?"

"D—d—da!" Stanislaw said, pointing toward the reeds. "There!"

Corey squinted. Lying by the stream was a body. And Corey once again remembered a crucial detail of his mother's story:

. . . just before he made his way through to civilization, he found the body of an armed Nazi soldier hidden in the bushes. To be safe, he took the man's pistol.

This was part of Stanislaw's destiny. But they already had a gun, and Stanislaw wouldn't be needing another. In the darkness, Corey could spot the faint amber glow of a settlement along the river. "Come," he said. "We're almost there. We're heading into friendly territory."

"Ja, the Resistance," Stanislaw said. "Kurtstadt. I know this. I—I want them to see me walk on my own."

"Are you serious?"

Drawing himself up, Stanislaw yanked his arm off Corey's shoulders. He took a few deep breaths, his eyes trained forward. And he began to walk. "The ground is level," he said. "I am serious."

Corey couldn't help but smile. Stanislaw was a bear of a man.

"Okay, I'm going to tell you something really important," Corey said as they approached the village. His mom's story was racing through his thoughts like a chyron. "Um, just a thought. Remember, the Resistance fighters are all over the place. Some of them are pretending to be Nazi sympathizers, to trap the Nazis themselves. So if we see a car with a swastika, it may be them."

Stanislaw nodded. "So we are careful, yes? We do not shoot?"

"Exactly," Corey said with relief. "Just hide and let them go by."

Corey looked at his watch. It was nearly three in the morning. He could see a lone streetlamp now along a dirt road, casting a sickly yellow light. A distant rumble sounded from their left.

But this was the puttering of a slow-moving car, its headlights dimmed. It wasn't a convoy. Just one car. One car about to pass two total strangers on the road in wartime. It would be risky to just stand there. It was a better idea to lie low, wait for it to pass, and then continue to Kurtstadt. Corey glanced at Stanislaw, then eyed a thick copse to his left. "We hide there?" Stanislaw asked.

"Yeah," Corey said. "But no shooting."

They slipped into a deep ditch beside the road. There, they hid behind a bush and kept silent as the car slowly rolled past. There were no swastikas. It wasn't a grand black Nazi sedan, just an old Mercedes. The windows seemed black in the darkness. But the front passenger-side window rolled down as the car pulled closer. It stopped right in front of them and a man in a plain tweed coat called out, *"Hallo? Wer ist da? Hallo? Wir haben uns verlaufen!"*

"Good hiding skills," Stanislaw said.

"What are they saying?" Corey asked.

"They're lost."

"Do you trust them?"

Stanislaw was shaking. "I don't trust anybody. I left

a Nazi guard unconscious in the woods."

Now the driver was stepping out of the car. He was heavyset and wore a plaid cap. He had a puffy pink face and a broad smile. *"Grüß Gott!"* he called out. *"Bitte, können Sie uns helfen?"*

Corey stood tentatively, peeking up over the ditch. "I don't speak German," he said.

"Und dein Vater?" The driver was looking toward where Stanislaw was hiding.

Corey's great-uncle stood slowly. *"Onkel, nicht Vater.* He thinks I am your father." He answered the man stiffly in German. As the conversation continued, the driver's smile never faded. But Stanislaw seemed to get more and more agitated. "They want to see our papers," he said.

"What?" Corey shot back. "I don't have papers. Who are they anyway?"

Stanislaw shrugged. "This man says that one of the passengers in the back wants to talk to you. He knows you."

Corey laughed. "I seriously doubt it."

At that moment the rear window rolled down. It revealed a man wearing a floppy black hat and a shabby trench coat. He was also wearing sunglasses, which seemed a little ridiculous considering the hour.

Corey leaned in. "Hey, I'm Corey. Sorry, but I'm new here. I don't know German. Just walking to town with my uncle."

A heavily accented German voice answered, "They want me to kill you."

"What?" Corey said, recoiling.

"But I want to see you up close. It is amazing, *mein Junge*. You have not aged. Not a day."

As the man removed his sunglasses, Corey found himself staring into the cold, bloodshot eyes of Adolf Hitler.

31

"**M**ein *Gott*."

Stanislaw backed away from the car. His leg collapsed beneath him, but he managed to stay upright.

Corey felt frozen in place, holding Hitler's glare. In the years since 1908 those eyes had lost any softness and doubt. They had hardened into an evil bloodlessness, sucking in the light around them. His face had sagged into crevices like stone. Corey knew that if he blinked even once, if he allowed even a morsel of fear, this man would reach into him and yank out his soul.

In that moment Corey knew Hitler's evil genius. In one statement Hitler had tried to own him. He'd said I know you. I am not shocked you are here. Not even time travel is more powerful than I am. All of that in four words:

You have not aged.

"Well," Corey said, "you have."

Out of the corner of his eye, Corey saw movement farther down the road. In the distance, a line of cars approached with lights out. As they came near, Corey could make out the image of a white-and-black figure. A swastika.

The convoy. The disguised Allies.

Hitler broke Corey's glance and turned toward the cars, too. He muttered one word softly to the others, and both doors of the Mercedes flew open.

As two soldiers jumped out, Stanislaw pulled out his gun. "Zurück, Corey!" his great-uncle screamed. "*Get back!*"

Corey jumped into the ditch, tumbling to the snowy ground. For the first time since they'd left the hut, he felt the pain of the back injury from Vienna.

Stanislaw let off two shots. One of the Nazi soldiers howled in pain, dropping his rifle and falling to the ground. Crouching behind the vehicle, the other soldier took a potshot at Stanislaw that went way over his head.

Hitler's window rolled up, and Stanislaw shot again.

The bullet cracked the Führer's window but bounced off. "Bulletproof glass," Corey said. He had no clue it had been invented yet.

As Stanislaw blasted the windshield of the Mercedes into fragments, Hitler let out a frightened squeal in the back seat. Now the convoy was moving closer. For a moment Corey's heart lifted. With so many Allies disguised as Nazis, the Mercedes didn't stand a chance. And neither did Hitler.

A distant shot rang out from one of the cars, then another. Corey could see the third shot slicing through the air in front of his eyes. All of them flew way over the top of the Mercedes. Now the driver was screaming something into a walkie-talkie in German, and an answer crackled over the line.

The convoy picked up speed. More shots flew, but none of them seemed aimed at the Mercedes. And the soldier was gesturing toward Corey and Stanislaw.

They were following his instructions.

"They *are* Nazis!" Corey shouted.

"Aaaagh!" Stanislaw shrieked, as a bullet hit him in the arm.

As the big guy collapsed, Corey ran toward him. He crouched as low as he could. Behind him, one of the soldiers in the Mercedes was frantically opening the car's trunk. It was loaded with explosives.

"They must be ambushing the town," Corey said.

"That is what they think," Stanislaw said, struggling to his knees.

Now the remaining soldier was reaching into the back seat to pull Hitler to safety. "The coward," Stanislaw muttered. "He lets everyone else do the fighting for him."

Stanislaw fired at the soldier, the shot grazing his arm. As he fell away, an explosive flew over Corey's head from the convoy. It hit the ground, sending up a spray of dirt. In the back seat of the Mercedes, Hitler was screaming. Corey dived into the door, slamming it shut. He crawled his way to the back of the Mercedes, to the open trunk. The only thing he even vaguely recognized was a hand grenade. He'd seen those on TV. Crouching, he snatched one from the trunk, pulled the pin, and tossed it toward the caravan.

It exploded on the road, digging a violent-looking pothole.

As Corey spun around, a bullet whizzed over his shoulder, directly between him and Stanislaw. He leaped to the ground in the other direction and rolled away. He was on the other side of the car now. There, the first soldier Stanislaw had shot was flat on his face, not moving.

"Stanislaw?" Corey called out.

"*Pass auf*, Corey!" his great-uncle called from the other side.

"What does that mean?" Corey replied.

His only answer was a click, directly above him. "It means," said a voice in a thick German accent, "watch out."

Corey turned, looking up into the barrel of a pistol.

32

Corey knew in a flash that a Throwback could die in the past. Because a bullet was a bullet, and flesh was flesh.

It was sheer physics.

But before he could react, the soldier's body jerked, as he were doing a sudden dance. His eyes never moved from Corey. He lowered his pistol slightly, then raised it again. With a nasty squint, he opened his mouth for one last statement. One last gloat.

But all that came out was a stream of blood.

With a last wheeze, the soldier fell to the ground, dropping his pistol. Corey crawled around the Mercedes to the other side. There, a few feet away, Stanislaw held a smoking gun.

"You—you did that?" Corey cried out.

"And now I will do something that I have been wanting to do for this whole war," Stanislaw said, reaching for the handle of the Mercedes's rear door. "*Guten Nacht*, Adolf!"

But before he could pull the door open, the rear window rolled down. The barrel of another pistol peeked through.

Stanislaw's eyes widened. He tried to jump away, but another shot caught him in the shoulder. He spun and fell to the ground again. Corey leaped after him, pulling him into the ditch. "Are you all right?"

From the caravan, a bottle-shaped missile flew directly toward them. An explosion sent up a geyser of dirt, not ten feet from them.

But Stanislaw's eyes were on something behind Corey. He whirled around to see Adolf Hitler running away, heading toward the Nazi caravan with one of the other soldiers who had been in the Mercedes. The caravan's lead vehicle, a nasty-looking Nazi truck, was stuck in the pothole Corey had made.

"Stay down, Corey!" Stanislaw said.

He let off a couple more shots toward Hitler, but they missed. The two other Nazi soldiers were lying in the dirt. Stanislaw sank to his knees. He dropped his gun and supported himself on his hand.

Corey turned to Stanislaw and pulled him away from the road. "Come on, we have to get out of the line of fire."

He ran toward a gully just beyond the road, pulling Stanislaw along. Staying low, they descended into it. Stray bullets whizzed way over their heads as they flopped down into a snowbank. "We have to get you to a hospital," Corey said.

Stanislaw reached for his gun and tried to scramble upward, but Corey yanked him down. "What are you doing?"

"I want to personally kill that monster!"

"Are you crazy?"

Corey wrestled the gun from Stanislaw's hand. Blood was oozing again from the head bandage, from his arm, from his shoulder. He collapsed against the side of the gully, breathing hard. Corey heard the sound of heavy footsteps on the road and gripped the gun with both hands.

Peeking over the top, he saw Adolf Hitler catching up to the caravan. At least five other soldiers, dressed in flak jackets with guns at the ready, were racing toward him.

Corey thought of shooting, but he knew they'd

both be killed in an instant.

He waited until the men ushered the Führer out of sight. In a few minutes they'd figure out how to get past the grenade hole, and the next stop would be Kurtstadt. "They're planning to blow up the village," Corey said.

"A spy . . . must have . . . told them . . . about the Allies . . . occupying the village," Stanislaw said through clenched teeth.

Keeping low, Corey pulled Stanislaw along the ditch, which followed the road toward Kurtstadt. By now, the noise had drawn a crowd. In a moment three Jeeps sped toward them, followed by a group of armed men running toward them. "*Was ist los?*" one of them called out.

Stanislaw, grunting through his pain, explained what had happened. The men listened, pointing the Jeeps toward the caravan. One of the men was picking up the wounded Nazi soldier from the road.

A strong-looking, sandy-haired woman in a heavy wool coat approached them. "I am Dr. Feder," she said, taking Stanislaw's other arm. "I will help you with . . ."

"Stanislaw," Corey said.

"We were not expecting an attack," she said. "If we

had not heard the noise, they would have arrived into Kurtstadt."

"They have . . . much explosives," Stanislaw said.

"Where did they get you?" Dr. Feder asked.

"My . . . left arm . . . and oh yes, my left shoulder," he said, turning to show the two growing bloodstains. "Just . . . a couple of small pieces."

Dr. Feder was now eyeing Stanislaw's head and ankle injuries too. She removed a bulky walkie-talkie from her belt and shouted something in German.

In a moment, one of the vehicles veered toward them. As it neared, Corey could see the Red Cross symbol of an ambulance. It screeched to a halt, and a team of workers scrambled to remove a stretcher from the back.

"Well then," Stanislaw said with a laugh. "Do I look that bad?"

Corey took a deep breath, eyeing the masses of deep-red stains that were growing together. "Honestly, you're a mess."

Stanislaw smiled. "No. No, Corey," he said. "I am the luckiest man in Germany."

33

Stanislaw was in such poor condition, Corey was surprised the hospital allowed a visitor.

The girl looked confused, and so fragile Corey was afraid she'd fall apart if she touched anything. Her eyes were hollow in their sockets, her hands spindly. If the doctors hadn't told him she was ten years old, he would have thought her to be a grandmother.

It felt rude to stare at her. She reminded Corey of someone. Maybe a younger version of some actress, he wasn't sure. He turned away. Like the girl, he stared at Stanislaw's motionless body.

The nurse who had ushered her into the hospital room asked Corey something in German, but he shrugged and said, "American."

"Ah." With a nod, she fell silent. But she didn't leave. Instead she stood protectively by the girl's side.

Stanislaw was moving in the bed now. He had been in a long, drugged sleep, his head and his left arm wrapped in fresh bandages, his leg suspended above the bed with a winch. As he turned, his eyes blinked for the first time in hours. "Grrrommmm . . . *wieder saaberrroff* . . . nnnnngahh."

Corey was sure that bore no relationship to German or English. But at the sound of his voice, or maybe at the sight of his battered features, tears began rolling down her cheeks. When she finally spoke, her voice was tiny and meek.

"Hallo?" was all she managed before choking back sniffles.

With a grunt, Stanislaw tried to sit up, but instead fell back into the mattress. "*Owwwww . . . der Schmerz . . .*"

"This means, the pain," the girl said, her voice barely over a whisper.

Corey glanced at her in surprise. Her English was refined, British sounding. "Thanks," he said. "I thought so."

Now she stepped closer to Stanislaw. With a slow gesture, graceful and sure, she touched his hand. His eyes were clenched, but the lids seemed to relax a bit.

"Du siehst ganz schön aus, Bruder," the girl said.

Stanislaw's eyes blinked open like they were on a spring. "Helga?" he said. "Bist du wirklich da, oder träume ich?"

Corey didn't know what any of that meant. But he recognized the only word he needed. A name.

Helga.

Helga Meyer, his mom had said, as she smiled at the old black-and-white photo of Mutti and her family, before she became Helga Velez.

"You're . . ." Corey said, but the words choked in his mouth.

The girl gave him a startled glance.

"You're my grandmother." The words left Corey's mouth before he could stop them. "What are you doing here?"

"Excuse me?" She flashed a frightened, unsure glance at Corey. "I—I was brought here. By the Resistance. They told of two heroes, who held off a Nazi attack. One, they told me, was an escaped prisoner. When they mentioned the name, Stanislaw . . ."

Corey nodded. The girl kept talking, but his thoughts were drowning out the words.

He knew this story. Helga—Mutti—had lived it. That was what his mom had said. Thin and weak, she was smuggled away by the Resistance, to a border town in Austria. From there they managed to smuggle her out of Europe entirely, to South America. That same day the Nazis ambushed the village, killing everyone. Blessedly Mutti was on her way to Brazil and then eventually to Puerto Rico. That's where she met Papi, where he was stationed in San Juan. It was love at first sight.

Kurtstadt was the border town.

Corey thought hard about Stanislaw's story. Mom hadn't mentioned a village. All she said was that Stanislaw had almost reached civilization, before he'd been killed by Allied soldiers in disguise.

But it made sense now. It wasn't a coincidence that Helga and Stanislaw ended up in the same place. Helga was smuggled to an Allied-controlled former Nazi border village. The Nazis were taking prisoners there, thinking the same village was under their control. How many possible sites were there? This had to be the one!

In the old story, Helga had never known that her brother died in the woods. Now she was here with him. Because Stanislaw hadn't been killed. He and Corey had intercepted the Nazis. And that had tipped off the village. Which had not been ambushed.

"Hello, how is our patient doing?" The voice interrupted Corey's thoughts. He looked up to see Dr. Feder entering the room.

"Dr. Feder," Corey said, "how many people are in Kurtstadt?"

She smiled, cocking her head at the odd question. "Ten thousand, I believe?"

The Nazis ambushed the village, killing everyone, his mom had said.

"Uncle Stanislaw saved ten thousand lives . . ." he murmured.

Stanislaw let out a wheeze that sounded like a laugh. "It was you, Corey," he rasped. "You did this. Helga and I thank you."

The sight of his little sister seemed to make Stanislaw's pain magically lift. He began talking, haltingly at first, and then a torrent of German words, spilling over one another. The girl's face seemed to grow redder, more radiant. She laughed and gave him answers that made him laugh, too.

Corey could not stop staring at the girl's face. He could see the resemblance of this smiling, smooth-face girl to the papery old woman bound to a wheelchair. Before Mutti's mind had begun to weaken, when she was married to Papi, she had smiled just like this girl. A broad, goofy smile that made her eyes shrink to crescent-moon slits. The way Helga was laughing, right now—the soft *hoo-hoo-hoo*—that never changed. Corey had grown up loving to hear that laugh.

It made him very happy now.

"This is my sister, Corey," Stanislaw said, his eyes rimmed with tears. "She was not home when the Nazis came for our family. One of the neighbors hid her for months. They were poor and could barely feed her. When the Resistance found out about her, they smuggled her to the closest safe village. Here."

"I know," Corey said.

Helga smiled. "My brother tells me you saved his life. If not for you, I would not have found him here." Now she took Corey's hand in hers. It must have been frail and cold, but to Corey it felt warm and thick. To him at that moment it had the fragrance of Mutti's favorite perfume. It held the promise of dinners with mofongo and schnitzel, gifts from Puerto Rico and Germany, where she and Papi traveled every year. "How can I ever repay you?" she said.

The words caught in Corey's throat. "You . . . you will. Many times."

"Maybe you give me a list? I will do everything on it."

Corey smiled. "Tell your brother to come to New York," Corey said. "I have a feeling that if he does, you two will see a lot of each other."

"Yes," Helga replied. "Yes, I will!"

"And both of you, the minute you hear about a company called Apple, buy stock," Corey said. "Promise?"

Helga gave her brother a wry glance. "This boy is very strange. I like him."

"Me, too," Stanislaw said.

Corey burst out laughing. One by one, the others in the room joined him.

Laughter, he realized, was infectious. And some infections were helpful in a hospital.

It was great to have something to look forward to.

34

The back of the hospital stank so badly Corey nearly ran away. He held his breath, hiding behind a dumpster full of hospital waste. This was the only place where no one would see him. The streets of Kurtstadt were still chaotic after the morning's action.

Corey fished the coins out of his pocket and squeezed hard. He was a little afraid about returning to the present. Leila would be mad at him. But he was excited, too. When he returned to the present, everyone's memory will have adjusted. They would know who Stanislaw was. Mutti would never have grieved over her beloved brother. Maybe she would not have sunk into the depression that haunted her for so long.

In the meantime, Kurtstadt did not fall to the Nazis. Thousands of lives were saved.

Corey took a deep breath. He wanted more.

He looked for the hundredth time at his hands and feet. He touched his cheek. He had no symptoms at all.

Being a Throwback, he realized, meant helping the world one step at a time. Artifacts were all over the place. You had to keep going back. If you chose where to go, if you knew your limits, you could do it. You could avoid the chaos loop.

Corey knew he was not finished with Hitler.

But he was definitely finished with these dumpsters.

Squeezing his coins, he closed his eyes tight.

Owwww.

Ow, ow, ow, ow, ow, ow.

Tight. So tight. Confined like a size two straitjacket on a size twelve body.

This was different.

This was not like any time hop he'd experienced.

He wanted to scream. He wanted to get back to Kurtstadt and try again. What was happening? What had gone wrong?

He felt stuck. His body seemed to disintegrate and then snap together, again and again in microsecond bursts. He was surrounded and stranded, people and cities rushing by. Whirring machines engulfed him and disappeared in nanoseconds, and he spun among vast networks of orbiting globes like molecules. Buildings passed right through him at rocket speed, as howls high and low assaulted his ears. He sensed his brain separate from his nose, his arm light-years away from his chest, his feet in a different era than his eyes. He felt like he could tap a butterfly in the Jurassic Age and kick his feet onto George Washington's desk.

He felt squeezed in the limbo between past and present, the place where flesh and spirit were never meant to go.

Stop!

He hadn't questioned time travel. It had always just happened. Papou had described it to him as like bending space. Like closing the gap between distant galaxies. But what if you went too far? What if you were caught at the edge of space-time? What was there—a black hole?

Was this what death felt like?

Like you were exploding out into the universe,

spinning away from your own soul, atom by atom?

He didn't want to die like this. *Why wasn't it working this time?*

Corey opened his mouth to scream, but everything went black.

35

When Corey's eyes opened, he was in a room. Somehow he knew where this place was. But everything looked weird. Elongated. Too clear. It was as if his eyes had expanded to include the views from either side of his head.

It was Leila's room. Or some fun-house-mirror version of it.

Corey tried to sit up, but he couldn't. He was face-down, and all he could manage was a kind of modified push-up.

"Leila!" he called out. But his voice sounded muffled and odd, and about an octave too low.

He took a deep breath and called her again, louder.

He heard footsteps padding in the hall. He backed

away from the door and looked up. The door unlatched and slowly opened. For a moment he saw Ms. Sharp's friendly smile, and it made him feel warm and welcome after the crazy trip.

"Is Leila here?" Corey asked.

But she looked down, startled. Her eyes grew wide and her jaw dropped. It was pretty exaggerated, like a scene from a horror movie, and for a moment Corey wondered if he was supposed to laugh.

But her shriek was loud. And real.

She slammed the door. Corey could hear her racing down the hallway, screaming about 911.

Corey walked to the door, but before he could try the knob, it opened again and Leila rushed in.

"Oh. Dear. God," she said, putting her hand to her heart.

"Hey," Corey said. "What's up with your mom?"

She came into room and slammed the door behind her. "Corey. Don't say anything. We need to go, before Mom has a heart attack."

Before Corey could reply, Leila grabbed the blanket off her bed and threw it around him. Corey felt himself rising off the floor. She was lifting him—completely lifting him into her arms. "How are you doing this?" he cried out. "Put me down!"

He tried to shake loose, but Leila cried out, "Stop that!"

"Will you please explain what's happening?" Corey asked.

"For God's sake, Corey," she replied. "*Look!*"

She flung the blanket off Corey's head, enough so that he could see the mirror on the back of Leila's door.

At first he thought it was a trick. Leila was cradling what looked like a real gray wolf.

A memory jammed its way into his brain. His mom's story about Corey's grandmother:

"She lost all her family . . . when they were taken by the Nazis. . . . She was smuggled away by the Resistance . . . out of Europe entirely, to South America . . . and then eventually to Puerto Rico. That's where she met Papi, where he was stationed in San Juan. It was love at first sight."

But Mutti hadn't lost all her family! Her brother Stanislaw had survived. He was there to take care of her, at a small Resistance village near the Austrian border. A village that was supposed to be destroyed shortly after they sent her away.

The breath caught in Corey's throat.

Of course. Stanislaw was there to protect her. Which meant she never had to sail across the Atlantic with total strangers.

Which meant she never went to San Juan.

Never met the handsome, heroic Puerto Rican soldier named Luis Velez.

And never had a daughter.

Who never married a Greek-American man named Vlechos, aka Fletcher.

Who had never given birth to a son named Corey.

When the genes are confused by time travel, Papou had said, *they shift.*

Corey's face was covered again. He felt himself moving in Leila's arms, down the wood floor of the Sharps' apartment. He heard earsplitting, panicked screams from Leila's mom. He felt himself bumping downstairs, and then the cold of the New York City night.

As the sounds of the street gave way to the quiet of Central Park, Corey began to squirm. "Hold still," Leila demanded. "This is weirding me out."

"You? How do you think I feel?" Corey asked.

"Look, I'm not supposed to know you," Leila said. "I mean, to me, you should be a stray wolf in New York City. I should be scared like my mom. But I know that you are Corey, who lives around the corner from me. Even though technically you weren't born and I never met you."

"Your memory . . ." Corey grunted. "It didn't adjust."

"Exactly," Leila said.

"Why?"

"I don't know!" Leila said. "So I'm taking you to Smig. And Auntie Flora. They are much smarter than me. They've been through this. I will make them solve this problem. I will get back to you if I die doing it."

Corey saw the trees and the grass. His eyes focused on the dogs at the end of their leashes, the mother raccoon and her cubs in the hollow of a tree, a family of rats scurrying into a hole in the road.

He threw back his head and let out a loud, pitiful howl.

More adventures by
PETER
LERANGIS!

MAX TILT SERIES

THROWBACK SERIES